on the Rocks

MURPHY BR✤THERS #2

# Irish on the Rocks

## MURPHY BR🍀THERS #2

# MAGAN VERNON

Entangled Publishing, LLC
2614 South Timberline Road
Suite 105, PMB 159
Fort Collins, CO 80525
rights@entangledpublishing.com

Embrace is an imprint of Entangled Publishing, LLC.

Edited by Candace Havens
Cover design by Kelly Martin
Cover photography by
maglara/DepositPhotos,
jag_cz/DepositPhotos
Valentin Agapov/ Shutterstock
Nazar Skladanyi/ Shutterstock

Manufactured in the United States of America

First Edition September 2018

*embrace*

*Dedicated to my agent, Stephanie.*

*For always believing in me, even when I didn't believe in myself. Slainte.*

.

# Chapter One

The only things good about a charity gala were the free drinks and raising money for the less fortunate. Something I was taking full advantage of—the drinks, that is. Especially when my "date" was late and I didn't know a single soul in the place. I tried smiling and nodding to a few people, but the only conversations I'd had in months were with my family and my dog. Though, to be fair, she was pretty vocal and a better conversationalist than most of the men I'd dated.

At least I finally had a night out of the house. After staying with my mum and grandparents for the past month, the only time I ever left was for job interviews that never panned out.

But tonight, I got to be the girl in the red dress. The one that made my arse look good. Too bad I didn't have anyone to impress, including my best mate and "date," Sean.

Pulling my phone out of my pocketbook, I sent him a quick text.

Me: *Where the hell are you?*

Sean: *Just finishing up practice.*

Me: *Really? That's what you're going with?*

Sean: *Don't get your knickers in a twist.*

Me: *Are you really at practice or in some poor woman's bed?*

Sean: *Can't a man do both?*

I rolled my eyes, grabbing a drink from the bar and taking a large swig. Sean Murphy had been one of my best friends since we were in nappies, spending our summers together on my granddad's estate and our years being crazy in boarding school.

Now, I stood in the grand ballroom, alone, waiting for him and really wishing I had my dog there to talk to.

I took another big gulp of my drink.

Mum and I moved from the UK to Dublin a month ago, after her and my wanker of a father's year-long divorce battle ended. She had wanted to save face and I, at twenty-three, found myself laid off from my job and out of options.

"Champagne? Is there going to be a toast?" I asked to no one in particular when I finally noticed what I was drinking, staring at the glass as if it would answer me back.

"What would they toast to at a benefit for childhood cancer?" a husky voice responded, and I turned, wide-eyed, to see a man leaning on the bar next to me.

I'd recognize those dark blue eyes anywhere. Jack Murphy, now older with a tailored suit that molded to his well-defined frame, stared at me with his chiseled jawline and dimpled smirk. The one I'm sure had most girls dropping to their knees and begging for his attention.

Every girl but me, that is. Even if I did have a wee crush on the guy back in the day. I'd known him my entire life, and he always thought the sun rose and set on his shoulders. A very nice set of broad, manly shoulders, but that wasn't the point.

"Right. I guess that wouldn't make any sense," I muttered, taking a big gulp of bubbly and hoping I wasn't going to be knackered. No way could I miss my morning walk with Jane Pawsten, my Brussels Griffon, due to a hangover.

"How about I get you a different drink? Something Irish?" His smile turned into a half-cocked grin that I wasn't sure if I wanted to kiss or kick off his face. Had he lost his mind? With our past, I was surprised he was being so civil.

"Not much for whiskey, and I think this will be my first and last drink, but I'd settle for tea if they have that."

Okay, so it was my second, but I didn't want him to think I was a lush as I grinned, twirling the stem of my glass.

"Tea? I do enjoy a good cuppa as much as the next person, but when there's an open bar, I don't think they carry hot water or anything more than Lipton."

I laughed, even though the statement wasn't really that funny. Blast, I was a horrible flirt. And why was I even trying with him? Especially since I'd known this man all of my life but now he looked at me as if he didn't know who I was.

"So…what have you been up to lately? World domination and all that, I guess?"

Bollocks, I really was bad at this small talk. I also wasn't exactly sure what the oldest Murphy had been doing since I last saw him eight years ago. Sean didn't really talk to me about his brothers, but I knew his da had passed and Jack and his brothers had yet to take over the company. Something that I definitely wasn't about to bring up.

He laughed. "Running a pub franchise isn't world domination. Makes me sound like an evil villain from the comics when you put it that way."

Slowly he leaned forward in his seat, and I inhaled his manly scent of leather and mint.

Need pooled low in my stomach.

Where was my Sean buffer when I needed him?

"I read a book once where you thought the man was the villain the entire time but in the end, he was the hero," I blurted, wishing I had something better to talk about than what I had edited for freelance work.

He raised an eyebrow. "Don't think I've ever read something like that. Do you work in the publishing industry? Romance author? Or maybe you're a cover model?"

I choked on my own spit and let out a wheezing cough, putting my hand to my chest as I blinked rapidly. Why was he being nice to me? And why was I being nice back? "I'm in editing right now. Freelance for the time being. But if you know a publisher who is looking for a new editor, I'm all ears since my last one downsized."

He laughed, shaking his head. "Can't say that I know any publishers, *mo gra*, but if I knew the one who let you go, I'd boycot all of their books."

I struggled not to roll my eyes. "That's a horrible come-on. I would think after all these years you'd have something better."

He blinked, swirling the liquid in his rocks glass. "Hey, I was just trying to be nice. You see a girl sitting alone in a beautiful red dress and you buy her a drink and have a conversation."

His voice was smooth, laying it on thick with a dimpled smile as he leaned on the bar.

"I'm Jack, by the way, if I didn't say that before. Jack Murphy. But surely we've met before. I feel like I've seen you somewhere," he said, taking my hand in his.

I grazed my fingers along his and stared at our intertwined

digits. He couldn't be serious, could he? I hadn't changed that much since we were in boarding school. Yes, I learned how to tame my curls, got rid of the glasses, lost a few pounds, and had braces in Uni, but surely he knew the girl he was talking to. I'd been one of his brother's friends.

Or did he?

Oh, this was going to be good.

"Yes. It's nice to see you again, Jack. Been a long time," I said with a large grin.

His lips quirked into a half smile as he took a long sip of his drink. His eyes burned into me like he was still trying to figure out who the hell I was.

"Yes. It has been a long time. How's your family?" he asked, the generic question everyone asked.

Before my parents' divorce battle that left Mum with nothing. But I wasn't going to bring that up to the smiling man across from me. Oh no. I had a better idea.

"The family's grand. How's yours? Saw Connor was recently married and Sean's still playing rugby. Who would have known the little punk rock kid would turn into an athlete?" I laughed, taking a swig of my drink before setting it on the counter only to have it filled again by the bartender before I could protest.

Anyone would know about Connor's marriage and Sean's career if they lived in Dublin and were familiar with the Murphy clan. But not everyone would know the whole past. Jack's forehead crinkled slightly. He was still trying to place me.

*Oh, come on now.*

"All grand here," he said, turning to the bartender and ordering a refill of his drink. "It's been a very long day, and I'm about ready to head out of here." His blazing blue eyes searched mine.

"I get that maybe we've both changed a bit and haven't

seen each other since you graduated school. But you know, the night is still young. Why not stay and chat with me?" I tugged at the low neckline of my dress where his eyes briefly flitted to. We had changed since I last saw him, but I guess some things were still the same.

"When you put it that way, *mo gra*, how could I say no to another drink?" he asked softly. But the wheels were turning as his brow quirked slightly.

I'd be lying if I said heat didn't flutter low in my stomach, and I had to push it back. He couldn't just use cute little Irish terms of endearment and expect me to bow down to him. Especially when he didn't even remember me.

"It's no tea, but I guess I can settle for this champagne. I just might need to call a cab home. First drink I've had in months," I rambled.

He traced the lines of my hand, the light touches flickering feelings I thought had been burnt to the ground along with any thoughts of a relationship after my parents' divorce. "And why is that? Busy with work? Something else?"

I shook my head, setting my glass down before pulling back and letting out a deep breath. No. No. Just because he looked at me with those dark blue eyes and flashed his dimpled smile, didn't mean I could get personal with him. He may have just been asking a simple question, but one more drink and I'd forget that the arsehole didn't remember me. That I was just playing around with him.

"You know, I should actually probably head out, too. I haven't seen my friend who I'm meeting and I'm wondering if he's even going to show at this late hour."

I searched the room, seeing if maybe Sean had made a grand entrance, but no such luck.

He reached for my hand again, squeezing it gently. "Any man who would stand you up didn't deserve your attention in the first place."

I tried to pretend like I was a strong woman who wasn't affected by his words, but I totally was. My heart beat rapidly in my chest like I'd just run a marathon. The alcohol was affecting me more than I realized. No way could I still be attracted to Jack after all these years.

I shook my head, a slight smile crossing my lips as I tried to ignore the heat rising in my neck. "You're just saying that."

He grinned. "A woman like you, seeing just how far you can push me before I admit that I don't recognize you, is definitely not someone I would just say anything to for shites and giggles."

I furrowed my eyebrows. "So you admit you have no idea who I am."

Blast that damn distracting dimple. "I have some idea that we went to school together. But I don't think I could forget a girl like you."

"Are you talking about my tits or my attitude?"

He laughed, shaking his head. "You're a real gas, I'll give you that. And the most interesting person I've talked to in a long time."

"Is that so?" I couldn't help putting my chin in my hand as I leaned forward, knowing full well that he was getting an eyeful of my chest popping out of my dress.

Before he could respond, the world moved in slow motion.

My elbow on the bar.

My arm hitting the full glass of champagne.

Said glass toppling over and all of the liquid contents now soaking into his probably expensive suit pants.

Gasps came from people pretending not to watch as Jack stood up, the champagne now running all the way down his pant leg.

"Ah shite," I yelled and turned to the bartender who already had a towel in his hands.

Quickly I knelt down, pressing the cloth to Jack's leg and

not noticing how far my hands had traveled until he let out a low groan and I saw the very hard bulge staring me in the face.

"Grace."

My eyes widened as I popped my head up to meet his stare. "You knew it was me?"

He grabbed the towel, trying to pat the pool of liquid that had situated itself right near his groin.

The exact spot I was almost touching.

My face heated as I stood up, now realizing how much of an arse I had just made of myself.

He sighed, shaking his head. "I didn't at first. You've cleaned up a bit since our school days, but it didn't take long. I just wanted to see how long we could play this game. I didn't see you throwing a drink on me."

I put my hands on my hips, the embarrassment now gone and anger seething through me. "I didn't throw anything on you. It fell. An honest mistake."

"Oh, horse shite. We both know your little sexy act to get me to stare at your tits was an excuse to knock that drink over."

"You are overreacting."

He rolled his eyes, giving up and tossing the wet towel back on the bar before downing the rest of his drink and setting the empty glass back where he found it. "I'm just calling it a night. Say 'hi' to my brother when he gets here, will ya?"

Before he could leave me standing there looking like a fool, I grabbed my purse, not wanting to be the one left standing there. "You're absolutely maddening. Did you know that?"

He smirked. "I've been called worse."

I didn't even bother saying goodbye as I turned on my heel and headed in the opposite direction, looking for the nearest exit.

I didn't care that I hadn't seen Sean yet, or that people were gaping open mouthed at me.

The night was definitely over, but I had a feeling I was in for a lot more trouble in Dublin.

• • •

Sean: *So…wanna tell me what happened with you and my brother?*

I rolled my eyes at Sean's messages that I received at the unholy hour of three a.m. when I was already in bed.

Me: *Nothing happened with me and Jack. Just him being an arse after a stupid mistake. I went home right after that, which is more than I can say for you.*

Sean: *Hey, I did show up and you were already gone.*

Me: *Whatever.*

Sean: *LOL you know I love you. How about we hang out today? Your mum having brunch? If there's sweets to go with tea, I'm in.*

I smirked, even though he couldn't see it. As kids, Sean and I bonded over our mutual love of sweets that we'd sneak from Granddad's stash he hid from Grandmum.

As we got older, his love of food turned him into a strapping man with legs like tree trunks, perfect for a professional rugby career.

But I, on the other hand, would get a whiff of a Galaxy Bar and gain ten pounds.

A healthy regimen of watching what I ate and the treadmill helped to take off the baby fat, but the scars from the bitches in boarding school still remained, and so did the curvy hips.

Me: *You can even have my scones if you promise never to leave me at a gala again.*

Sean: *I make no promises, but I will take those scones.*

Me: *See you at ten.*

For once, Sean was only five minutes late to my grandparents' house.

"No girls chasing after you this morning?" I asked, raising a brow as the butler let him into the house.

He was dressed in his Sunday best with a three-piece suit hugging his barrel chest and wide shoulders and hiding the tattoos skating up and down his arms. The beard and styled hair added to his charming bad-boy look.

If I hadn't known the guy all my life and been best mates, I might have had a crush…like the one I harbored for Jack as a girl. And maybe still did? There was no way that anything was going to happen between us now. Not after I spilled champagne all over his probably very expensive suit and made an arse of myself. Even if I couldn't stop thinking about that cocky smirk. Damn him for being so cute.

"For tea and scones, I'll do just about anything," Sean said with a laugh and followed me through the foyer.

The house in the city was considered a downgrade from my grandparents' former country estate, but the place was still massive and filled with antiques and priceless oil paintings. We had to go down a long hallway, past two parlors, before we even got to the dining room.

The table was filled with enough food for an army yet only Granddad, Grandmum, and Mum sat at the table. Their faces lit up as soon as Sean walked in.

"Everyone, you remember Sean? He's here for brunch, even though he missed seeing me at the gala last night and he's terribly sorry," I said, side-eying him as we sat down in one of the upholstered high-back chairs.

"I remember him. He was the fat one who wore eyeliner." Grandmum pointed a crooked finger.

I snickered, watching Sean's face turn redder than the tomatoes on the sandwiches.

While Granddad was in a suit and Mum in a modest blazer and blue dress, Grandmum wore her usual eccentric attire of a feathered hat and lemon-yellow wrap dress that I was pretty sure had pugs printed on it. The older she got, the crazier her fashion choices were, and her filter was always hit or miss.

"It was a punk phase. We all had one," he muttered, taking a large bite of scone.

"And there's no one else I would have rather gone through my safety pins and mosh phase with than you," I teased.

"I think we still have a picture of that summer we let you two go to that place with the same name as a church. Granddad thought you were going to mass and figured he'd join," Grandmum went on, flitting toward the living room and returning with a leather photo album.

Sean laughed. "Ah, the St. Francis Xavier days."

Grandmum opened the book, flipping a few pages before setting it on the table and turning it toward us.

I snorted, picking up the old book and looking at the photos of us in our donkey jackets and Tam O'Shanter hats, standing outside the famous music hall.

We were surrounded by a thick layer of smoke but smiling with our thick eyeliner and chubby cheeks.

There were times I missed those days of being in our own little bubble, listening to music and forgetting the world.

"Didn't Sean's brother Jack have to pick you up that night

when Sean got into a tiff?" Mum asked, looking between the two of us.

Ugh, Jack. I didn't want to hear that name again.

Especially since Granddad and Mum didn't know what happened at the gala last night. They'd have a shite fit if they knew I spilled champagne all over the acting CEO of a company Granddad was on the board of.

"That was all Grace and her fisticuffs." Sean winked.

"Can we not talk about one of the most embarrassing moments of my life?" I muttered.

"As embarrassing as what happened with you and Jack last night?" Sean's eyes sparkled as he took a sip of his tea.

Bloody hell. I was going to get him for this.

"What happened with Jack?" Mum asked, her eyebrows raised high on her head.

"Nothing. Just a little mishap." I grumbled, glaring at my supposed best mate who was throwing me under the bus.

"You spilled champagne all over him." Sean barked out a laugh.

"Gracie," Mum chastised.

"It was a complete accident. I swear. I was talking and leaning in...and...oh bugger. I'm never leaving the house again," I muttered, taking a sip of my orange juice I wished was spiked.

No. Wait. Alcohol was what got me into this mess in the first place.

At this point I didn't need liquor, but maybe to disappear out back where one of the maids was running Jane Pawsten. At least the dog would never say anything to embarrass me.

Mum shook her head, but it was Granddad who spoke. "You probably owe him an apology. Even if it was an accident. We do work with him and our family has been friends with the Murphys for generations."

"I did apologize. Over and over again. And I still just

looked like an arse," I replied, trying not to whine with my strained voice.

"I'd actually love to see you have to grovel. And if I could film it then play it on repeat for whenever you're giving me shite, that would be grand, too." Sean laughed, and I groaned before polishing off my glass.

Apologizing at the event was one thing. But if I showed up at his office, begging for forgiveness, there was no way I wouldn't make a complete arse of myself...again.

Now I just hoped I wouldn't have to see Jack Murphy's sexy smirk for another eight years. Or however long it took him to forget me.

Again.

# Chapter Two

JACK

I lost the office pool a week ago.

My assistant, Fallon, was now married to my younger brother, Connor, and I had the under. Even worse, there was still this pesky little inheritance clause that I hadn't fulfilled my part of.

Thomas O'Malley's reading of the will was constantly in the back of my mind, the words replaying over and over.

*"After my death, my three sons, Jack, Connor, and Sean will each inherit their equal share of thirty-three and a third percent of the family franchise upon the day all three of their marriage certificates are certified by a priest and again by my solicitor Thomas O'Malley, six months after the day of their nuptials. If all three of them are not married within a year of my death, none will inherit, and the board may offer each son's ownership stake to the highest bidder."*

I had dozens of lawyers look for any loopholes that could get my brothers and me out of the blasted clause in Da's will, but none could do anything about it. Something about a damn "no-contest clause" in his estate planning. The only way we could get out of it was if the board voted us as Chief Executive Officer, Chief Financial Officer, and President.

Hell, even if they just voted me as CEO it would be grand.

But the board never agreed to anything that went against my father's wishes. Even if those wishes were insane. Which was weird because Da loved us and this business. Marriage should never have been a part of it.

So, my brothers and I continued to look for wives to keep the company in our family.

Yes, it sounded like arranged marriage shite from the 1700s but our Da was an old-fashioned man, as the family's solicitor liked to say. And now there was no getting out of it. I had to get married.

Instead of meeting my future wife at a gala, full of some of the most eligible women in Dublin, I ran into Sean's best mate and she spilled champagne all over my suit then tried to wipe it off.

She said it was an accident, even as her delicate fingers trailed dangerously close to my cock. But somehow I wasn't sure that was the case.

I sat in my office on Monday morning and looked at the text Sean sent me with the word "throwback."

Holy feck.

The photos on my screen were of a short, frizzy-haired girl with large wire-framed glasses, standing outside a concert hall with my brother. Grace before her transformation. Which is why I didn't recognize her at first.

She looked nothing like the sexy woman I was still thinking about. She definitely grew up these past eight years and damn, did she grow up well. But my mind had other things to deal with today.

I had to hire a new assistant fast.

I had a temporary one. The girl from accounting was good and kept up with it, but she despised me, probably counting down the days till she went back to her position in accounting.

It wasn't my fault I liked things a certain way.

But that's what happens when you're running a multi-billion-dollar company.

Bollocks. I still wanted to slap Connor upside the head for stealing Fallon. She was a fecking good assistant. Except for the fact they were so happy. Damn them.

Maybe I was a bit hard on the temporary assistant. She hadn't broken my one major rule: no feck ups.

Feck ups like hitting on your brother's best mate.

The inheritance clause had me twisted from the day it was read. But I still pushed forward with the company. I sought out new franchises in the U.S. and new charities to invest in, which helped raise our profile. That's not why I did it, but showing up for those galas had given us what the Americans liked to call creds.

One of my first acts as standing CEO was to hand over a hefty donation to a few charity organizations. One in particular held a gala for donors and to honor Da.

The night out was supposed to be my time to relax. Have a few drinks and maybe find someone to connect with. I didn't expect to spot the gorgeous doe-eyed girl or laugh like I hadn't in ages.

There had been something familiar about her and it took me longer than I cared to admit to look past the styled hair and ample amount of cleavage to realize it was Grace. The same girl, who last time I saw her, I saved from getting arrested when she got into a fight with some bird at a concert. Told the police I'd handle her, even though I left a date early to pick up the two unruly kids with their dark eyeliner and screaming music. She should have been grateful, but instead she just stuck out her tongue and ignored me the entire ride back to her Granddad's place.

I smiled, thinking of her in the back seat, her arms crossed over her chest and trying to appear pissed off at the world. But as soon as Sean cracked a joke, a broad smile would appear on her face.

Dammit. Why was I still thinking about her?

It was time to just forget about that smile and focus on the company and finding a wife.

"Mr. Murphy?" Aileen, the temporary assistant bellowed, cracking the door open.

Where was Fallon? She should have been back this morning to help find a suitable replacement

"Yes?"

"Fallon and Connor have headed to the meeting. Called your phone but you didn't answer," she said, her words monotone as if she was running on auto-pilot, practically just a voice message reading back to me.

"Feck," I muttered, standing up and sliding my phone into the front pocket of my jacket after checking the time. I did see a missed call, but she didn't leave a voicemail or send a text. That's what Fallon would have done.

But she wasn't Fallon. She didn't do the overkill that spoiled me. I probably needed to start doing more for myself in that department but not today. Not when I was running late.

"Have my calls go to voicemail while I'm out," I said as politely as I could before quickly making my way out of my office and down one of the wide hallways toward the conference room.

I raked my fingers through my hair, wondering how long the hiring process would be for a new assistant.

Should I even get a new assistant or just try and see how much I could do with something virtual? Maybe even see if I could just use some of the interns down in marketing. I made a mental note to check on that.

"Deep in thought?" Fallon asked as she rounded the corner, meeting me in the middle of the hallway.

"Just thinking about the meeting and how late I'm running. Think you could check in on how hiring is going for me down in HR?" I smiled at my sister-in-law as she adjusted the red frames of her glasses.

She laughed, shaking her head. "I think it's still the same. A ton of applicants, but none seem to make it through the vetting process. You wouldn't believe how many people can't pass a basic proofreading test."

I shook my head but offered a small nod to the beaming woman.

At first, I thought Connor was with my assistant to piss me off and get the company. But seeing the way he looked at Fallon, even now as he leaned against the wall near the conference room door, there was no doubt they were in love.

"Connor Murphy, first one to the meeting?" Fallon asked before he leaned over and kissed her cheek.

"Thought I was the last. No way in Hell was I going into a board meeting without my blond distraction, and you know, my beastly brother," Connor said, flashing a smug grin in my direction.

He was always a pain in the arse. Fallon even had to call and wake him up for a few meetings when he was working the Boston offices. She never told me he was running late, and always stood up for the lad, though I knew better.

"You know the board won't be happy with any of us for coming in late," I said, narrowing my eyes at my brother.

"Could be worse," he said, putting his hand on Fallon's back and his other hand on the door handle. "Could have not shown up at all and stayed on the honeymoon a few more days. Which I wouldn't have minded either."

Fallon stifled a squeal as he nuzzled her neck. Definitely not proper office behavior and her red face showed that as she pushed him away. But her bright smile also said she loved it.

Fecking honeymooners.

The board consisted of a little over a dozen people. Mostly older men who were at least in their sixties, if not seventies or eighties, and probably should have retired long ago.

But the one that stood out was the little old man with his silver cane, now hobbling as fast as he could toward me.

"Seamus. Good to see you're still well," I said, nodding slightly and trying to forget that I blatantly hit on his granddaughter.

He stopped, leaning against the wall slightly. "I wanted to tell you that I'm sorry about Grace. She's had a rough go of it lately. She meant no harm, and I deeply apologize for her actions."

I nodded, quirking my lips at the old man, but my mind was elsewhere. I needed my game face on for this meeting, so Connor, Sean, and I could show the board we weren't just some spoiled heirs.

We were a team who could run the company. Proposing one hundred new franchises within the next five years was a big undertaking that I had worked on tirelessly. Which was maybe why I hadn't recognized Grace.

"It's fine, Seamus. We all have our bad days." I clapped his shoulder, squeezing it gently.

"Well, you made one hell of an impression on her, at least. And if there's anything I can do to make up for her actions, you let me know, okay?" He raised his bushy eyebrows.

I smirked, thinking there was nothing the retired jeweler could do, but I'd humor him. "I will."

Connor and I took our seats next to the head of the board, who I was pretty sure was half asleep.

Sean showed up just as we were getting ready to start, taking the seat on the other side of me.

He smelled of sweat and grass, the collar of his rugby uniform visible under his suit.

"Miss anything good?" he whispered.

"We're just getting started," Connor said, holding up the remote to start the first slide.

There was no way the board could say no to this endeavor.

• • •

I'd spent the past week contacting commercial real estate brokers with quotes on possible land deals. Connor and I had laid the foundation, but I wasn't going to bother him on his honeymoon to help me out while I prepared the finishing touches.

How many sleepless nights had gone by while Connor was gone? I hated to say it, but having him and Sean work with me was the best partnership I could have asked for. With Connor back and maybe Sean willing to step up, I could have time for other things.

Like finding a wife.

Grace's face flashed through my mind. The way her lips curved in a pout as she tried to help wipe the offending liquid off my pants, but instead had me more than rising to the occasion. Maybe I was too much of an arse for what was probably an accident. And now I had no way to apologize. I couldn't just show up at her flat or wherever she was staying. That would be rightfully creepy.

No. I just had to get her out of my mind and move on with the business.

• • •

"Are we going to talk about what happened with you and

Grace?" Sean whispered as we shook hands with the board members before they went down the line to Fallon and Connor.

"Not right now," I muttered, nodding my head in the direction of the beaming old men, hobbling on their canes.

"They probably can't hear us, but okay. We'll talk later," he said with a grimace.

The men congratulated Connor and Fallon on their nuptials, but probably secretly hoped it had never happened so the clause could still stand. The shite Fallon's ex-boyfriend pulled at the ceremony almost made the whole thing fall apart.

"Connor, my boy. Fallon. Good to see that nothing derailed the two of you in holy matrimony," Seamus said, wobbling toward us and shaking both Fallon and Connor's hands then nodding at Sean and me.

"Thank you. Isn't there some saying about a rough start means smooth sailing?" Connor said with a grin, glancing in my direction.

Seamus nodded solemnly. "I do hope so. I was just about to apologize to Jack again for my granddaughter's behavior. As I told him earlier, she and her mum have had a rough go of it. She's been here in Dublin for over a month and still hasn't found a job in publishing. She's a former editor at one of those big publishing houses in London, you know?"

"Oh?" Connor asked, glancing at me out of the corner of his eye.

"Just a little mix-up. But I hope Grace wasn't too offended. And she's all right. I should really take her to lunch or something to apologize for my behavior, too," I said, trying to hide my grimace.

Connor winked in my direction before looking back at the old man. "You know, Jack is looking for an assistant. If your granddaughter can keep him in line, she'd be perfect for the position. You should tell her to apply and we could get her scheduled for an interview."

My ears burned and I stepped forward, clasping my brother's shoulder. Of course the gobshite would do that.

"That's not necessary. I'm sure Grace is far too overqualified for an assistant position and wouldn't even be interested."

Sean laughed, clapping his hands together. "Even if she isn't, I'd love to see the look on her face if she made it through HR and the vetting process, only to have to face you again in the interview."

Fallon smiled, stepping to closer to the old man. "We could really use someone who can proofread, and there would be plenty of room for her to move up in the company. Since I'm helping Jack out with the interviews, I'd love to meet her, even if she decides she doesn't want the job. Please extend the offer. And if you have her email address, I'll send her a request myself."

This time I did glare at the sweetly smiling Fallon as she took down Grace's email before helping to lead Seamus out of the conference room.

I owed it to the old man, I knew that. He was one of my father's closest friends and he'd always been good to my brothers and me. Not to mention his granddaughter was bloody gorgeous. But I'd had beautiful women outside my office door as my assistant before and none ever lasted long. I couldn't rightfully fire the girl then look at her grandfather in every board meeting.

Once Seamus rounded the corner and it was just the four of us Murphys standing in front of the room, I turned to Connor and Fallon. "What the hell do you think you two are doing?"

"Helping you out. You need an assistant and she needs a job." Connor frowned.

"I agree. Though I hope I can get to Seamus's place before she gets that email so I can see the look on her face," Sean said with a laugh and was gone before we could say anything else.

I sighed, raking my hands through my hair before glaring at Connor and Fallon. "You two can't offer an interview to a girl you don't even know anything about. HR has to go through a process."

Connor smirked. "Someone with editing experience could pass a few tests then be up in your office for an interview in no time. Unless there's a reason you wouldn't want to hire her. Have a past tryst that you don't want Sean to know about?"

I straightened and cleared my throat. "Nothing ever happened like that with Grace and me. She's one of Sean's best mates. That's all."

"Okay. I believe you," Connor said, raising his hands. "But if there is something, might be worth persuing. The board wouldn't question a marriage between a Walsh and a Murphy, that's for sure."

I laughed slightly, shaking my head at the ridiculousness of it all. "Why don't I head to the jewelry store now? I'll pick up a ring and ask her to help fulfill the heir clause. Six months with me can't be too bad if she can get a reasonable divorce settlement."

For a while I actually thought Connor and Fallon had that agreement, and maybe they still did. Though the way he smiled at her when I said that did seem like it had been discussed.

Connor shrugged. "I'm not telling you to do anything. You need an assistant. She needs a job. What's the harm in having her fill out the application? I'm not saying marry her. But maybe be open to something. For the company."

My jaw ticked. He knew exactly the words to say to me.

That all of this was for Murphy's. It wasn't about some office romance. Just a marriage for the company.

"Should I help Aileen schedule something? I'm sure she'd be happy to get back to the accounting department," Fallon piped up, the grin spreading across her face as she pulled out her phone.

Her eyes widened after she typed in a few things. "Damn. I was just being nice, but one search on this Grace girl and, I have to say, she's impressive."

I frowned, taking Fallon's phone. "Let me see what you're looking at."

Staring back at me was a professionally styled photo of Grace and those red lips. I scrolled past her face quickly before the others noticed me staring at those gorgeous brown eyes. Moving down the web page for "Grace Evans: Freelance Editor," I found her school and former job information. As well as references and quotes from authors with best-selling titles behind their names. I always knew she was bright, but I didn't expect this much. Maybe it couldn't hurt to call her in for an interview if she did indeed fill out the form.

After all, I didn't need to piss off any board members. It wouldn't be so bad having someone help me take on more of my own scheduling before she moved on to a new position.

And if I could get the chance to make up for my arsery, then even better.

I sighed. "If she does go through the application process, I'll call her former employers and set up an interview with Fallon. Would that make you two happy?"

Connor laughed. "For now."

# Chapter Three

GRACE

I should have been focusing on the current manuscript that was staring at me from the computer screen. The author had low-balled me, but I needed the money until I found a full-time job and a flat I could afford.

But there was something else about reading the fictional woman's budding romance that had me thinking about my lack of a love life.

When Jack and I talked at the gala, and dare I say flirted, something new sparked in me. All of those feelings I'd only read about in books bubbled to the surface. But it was short-lived. And I, of course, made an arse of myself, making the brooding man hate me more than he already did.

All of those years not seeing the oldest Murphy brother should have made me forget about his arsehole ways. The cocky bugger who wouldn't give anyone, including me, the time of day even though I was only three years younger. Hell, he would have probably laughed if I had tried to make a move the last time I saw him when I was sulking in the back of his swanky car.

But Saturday night he looked at me differently. That stupid little dimple popping on his cheek and he talked to me so warmly.

Then of course I had to go and ruin the little moment we had. Like always.

Mum had been mortified when she had heard the sordid details. Grandfather had said he would smooth things over at the Murphy board meeting today.

Frustrated, I decided to head to a little café down the road. Maybe a croissant and a cappuccino would get me back on track to finish this editing job. I also wouldn't have the added distraction of my dog begging for attention or Mum asking me questions when I was in the middle of a heated scene.

When the waiter had left the table after I placed my order, I pulled my phone out of my bag.

I figured checking my email for jobs and a little mindless web surfing couldn't hurt while I waited for my food. I mainly used all of my social media accounts for freelance jobs, so everything I pulled up was bookish and some friends from uni or boarding school.

This included Sean who had posted a photo from his brother Connor's wedding.

I couldn't admit, even to myself, that it wasn't the happy couple in the wedding photos that caught my eye. Jack Murphy's smolder practically blazed through the screen as he stood next to his brother.

He wore a suit tailored for his broad shoulders and tapered waist. Always clean shaven with a perfect hairstyle. The man never had a hair out of place, while I currently sat out in public wearing cropped yoga pants and a *What would Jane Austen do* T-shirt.

It would have been fine if I was going to yoga or the gym. But here I sat stuffing my face with croissant number two and thinking about what Jack was doing right then.

Bollocks.

I'll admit I thought about what would have happened if I hadn't made a complete fool of myself. One night with Jack Murphy would either be the ego boost I needed or the man would laugh as soon as he got me to his probably uber-fancy flat and saw me in my Wonder Woman knickers.

That is, if we would have even made it that far. It would have only been a matter of time before I had done something to mess it up. My parents' crazy divorce was always in the back of my mind, keeping me from any kind of romantic relationship.

Sure, the romance novels I edited had these grand love stories and I believed, yes, love and matrimony were great things. They just weren't for me.

I had seen what happened when love left a relationship. When, after being with someone for twenty-five years and having a child together, you just decide you want something different and fight tooth and nail to leave and take everything with you.

Watching my mum crumble, realizing that she had nothing after all of that fighting and more lawyer bills on top of it, crushed every notion I had of getting married.

She was the one who suggested we moved and help Grandmum and Granddad in Dublin. Not that I was sure they actually needed any extra with all of their hired hands. But I agreed, and together we would look to rebuild something in Ireland. As soon as we packed our bags for Dublin, I vowed, then and there, that I would never be in my mum's situation.

"Ma'am, your cappuccino," the waiter said, knocking me out of my own thoughts.

"Thank you," I said and closed out of social media, pulled

out my laptop, and tried to focus on work.

Even as I drank and ate, my thoughts still drifted to Jack.

There was always a little bit of a crush brewing inside of me for him. Even when I was just a little girl and first saw him, he was a gorgeous lad.

He'd aged even better. I'd seen some of the guys from his graduating class around social media. A lot were balding or rocking a dad bod without the kids.

Jack still had a full head of brown hair and what he was hiding under his suit, I was sure wasn't disappointing.

Quickly, I shook my thoughts away from what kind of boxers the man would wear. If I was lucky, I'd never see him, or his probably fancy, silky man knickers, again.

He was a busy man, after all. He had a company to run and I probably wouldn't be invited to another gala as Sean's date again. It was all just as well, though. I didn't think I could face Jack again.

After paying for my meal, and finishing a few chapters of edits, I grabbed my laptop bag and headed back to my grandparents where Grandmum was outside, picking weeds from the Delphiniums. Jane Pawsten barked at her heels and attacked each weed she threw on the ground.

"Grandmum, should you be bending over like that?" I asked, setting my bag down near the porch before crouching next to her and helping pick out a few of the lower weeds in the garden she couldn't reach.

She smiled. "Probably not, but the dog and I needed some fresh air. And between you and me and the fence post, those gardeners don't know what they're doing when it comes to my summer blooms. These are for the diligent worker."

She looked over her shoulder. "And Janey likes chasing the slugs out, so it's a win-win for both of us."

I laughed, watching the little dog attack one of the dead leaves like it was a ferocious creature. She barked and hopped on it a few times before she trotted over to me, nipping my hand until I gave her ears a good scratch.

Not only was my little dog vocal, but if one didn't listen to her, she'd find the first thing she could and chew it to a pulp. I'd gone through more pairs of shoes with her than I had in my entire life. I didn't think a ten-pound dog could do that much damage, but my favorite pair of black pumps said otherwise.

"I think you're starting to take a shine to Grandmum. Better not leave you alone with her too much or you'll have a new favorite person," I said.

She barked in response. Her little furry face was in need of a good grooming; her black beard looked more like Old Man Winter rather than the cropped look I preferred. But a groomer required money and someone like the woman in Notting Hill back home who could handle Jane's personality. I could have asked Grandmum and Granddad for a loan, but I didn't know if I'd ever be able to pay them back. And truth be told, the only thing I was sure of was that I needed to find a job that provided for myself and my dog. Other than that, I had no idea what the hell I was going to do.

"Has she eaten anything besides the weeds today?" I asked, looking at Grandmum whose red face barely showed underneath her large straw sunhat.

She sat back on her heels, rubbing her chin in thought. "I do remember the chef bringing us both eggs this morning. And I think we did have lunch. I had a sandwich, though I don't think Jane had that."

I shook my head. "You're getting very spoiled, little dog."

Grandmum nodded, petting Jane's ears. "It's nice to have her spunky personality around. Keeps me young."

"If she's ever a handful, you'll tell me? I can always take her with me when I go to the café or maybe even find a doggy daycare…"

I trailed, wondering how much longer I'd be able to afford the café trips or even a daycare if I didn't have a steady income.

Grandmum's hand went to mine, squeezing gently. "You don't have to worry about her, *mi cailín*, you need to take care of yourself."

"I'm doing all right," I muttered, trying to swallow the lump in my throat. I knew I couldn't hide anything from Grandmum. She was clairvoyant like that.

"You'd be doing better if you got out of this house once in a while."

I wrinkled my nose. "I was just gone all afternoon."

She waved her free hand. "I'm not talking about working down the street or one night out with that bearded boy, Sean. I'm saying, you need to find you a man. Like that Jack Murphy. You know the one you threw a drink on. He's a looker, if I do say so myself."

Heat rose to my cheeks and it wasn't just because of the summer sun. "Grandmum, first off, I spilled a drink. I didn't throw it on him. And secondly, I don't think there's any way a man like that would want to hang out with me."

She shook her head. "Jack's a fine boy. Maybe a little arrogant, but he does have a good heart. He'll come around and know your little slipup with a drink was nothing."

"I'm sure he's all of those things Grandmum, but really, I don't think I'll be seeing him again. Besides, I don't need a man to make me happy or get me out of the house." I tried to sit straighter. My bank account and lack of a life outside of my dog said I could use a date and a job, but it didn't need to involve me seeing Jack again.

She blew out a low whistle. "Now I know you modern girls have your toys that I've seen advertised online, but that can't substitute the real thing. And as far as I know those battery-operated things can't talk back. Though once I did see a documentary…"

I waved my hand, cutting her off before she started getting into anything deeper that would have me gagging from hearing the words from her lips.

"You know, I probably should get inside and feed Jane," I said, quickly standing.

Grandmum nodded, pointing a crooked finger at me. "Okay, but don't forget what I said."

I was afraid that her little "talk" was going to be burned in my memory forever.

Quickly, I scooped Jane Pawsten in my arms and grabbed my bag before we headed inside.

"Well that was interesting, Janey," I cooed, scratching behind her tiny perked up ears.

Her pink tongue darted out, licking at my hands with little puppy kisses.

"She's been barking since you left. So Grandmum volunteered to take her outside. Were they both okay out there? I'll make sure to send a maid out for her with some lemonade." Mum's shrill voice shuddered through me before she found the first poor house worker she could, making little overzealous suggestions at how she should serve the lemonade and what else Grandmum would need outside.

Mum meant well, but she had a tendency to go a little overboard with her helpfulness.

"I hope she doesn't give the maid relationship advice," I muttered, walking toward the large kitchen.

Opening one of the cupboards, I grabbed Jane's kibble, pouring it into a bowl and setting it beside her water bowl. The little dog happily buried her Wookie face in the dry brown food, crunching it so loud I swore it echoed off the walls.

"You were gone an awfully long time. Meeting anyone today?" Mum asked, raising her eyebrows.

I didn't even know she'd followed me until her voice rang in my ears.

Her too? Did everyone think I needed to be setup? Didn't they know what could happen at the end of a marriage if it didn't work out? Surely Mum knew better after all she went through. "I was working at the café. I left a note and told Grandmum before I left."

I wasn't a child anymore, but living with my mum and grandparents again made me realize just how much I was lacking.

I made a mental note to do another search for jobs later tonight. Maybe even search out in Cork if needed. Sure, the commute would be rough, but maybe it would build experience for a few months and then I could move onto something else.

"Work." She scoffed. "One hundred euros in a week isn't work, Gracie."

*And your job as an overbearing mum of an adult pays what?*

I smiled with a curt nod, even though I wanted to say something smart back. It wasn't fair, though. Mum knew she had nothing and probably didn't want her daughter to end up in the same position. But that didn't mean I had to sit and listen to her belittle me.

Pulling my phone out of my pocket, I aimlessly opened my email. I had it in my head I was going to pretend I had something to reply to. Then my eyes bulged when I saw a note from Jack Murphy c/o Fallon Murphy.

"Bloody hell," I muttered.

"What? Something wrong? Something on the face chat?"

I ignored Mum's comment and didn't bother correcting her. Instead, I opened the email, wondering what the hell he had to say via Fallon Murphy.

Wasn't that the name of Connor's wife? Not that I was

stalking his social media instead of working, but Granddad did say something about the new wife being Jack's former employee. Never knew it was actually the assistant. though.

I found myself smiling, thinking how that had probably ruffled his feathers. But my expression changed when I actually got to the heart of the email.

*Ms. Grace Evans,*

*We have an opening for an executive assistant position at Murphy's Pub Headquarters in Dublin. We were impressed by your background and would like to invite you to apply in our online system and then possibly sit down with you to talk a little more about the position.*

*Please let me know when you have gone through the application process and we can see about setting up an interview.*

*Looking forward to seeing you,*

*Jack Murphy*
*c/o Fallon Murphy E.A.455*

Why in the hell would I get an email like this from Jack or his assistant? His executive assistant who was also his sister-in-law? How the bloody hell did he even know I needed a job? Sean wouldn't have told him. Maybe…

Unless…

"Is Granddad here?" I asked Mum, not looking up from my phone and walking toward the dining room.

"Yes, he's in his study. Is everything okay, Gracie?" Mum asked, following closely behind me. "Sean stopped by earlier looking for you as well, smiling like he had a secret. Is there something I'm missing? Does this have to do with what happened at the gala? I may have had a talk with Grandfather, but didn't know if he said anything to Jack. Think he's interested in you?"

I ignored Mum, even though her words piqued my interest. We would have to have a talk about her and Grandfather meddling later. I opened the door at the end of the hall.

Granddad sat in his leather chair, the smoke from his pipe wafting in the air.

"Gracie. To what do I owe the pleasure?" He looked up from his newspaper with a broad smile.

"Did you happen to talk to Jack Murphy today?"

He nodded. "Ah. Did he get in touch with you?"

I swallowed hard, trying to control the shudder rising up my spine. "I just got an email from his assistant about a position opening and suggesting that I should apply."

Mum clapped her hands, before flitting into the room. "That's wonderful news. Is there an interview? Do you have anything to wear? Do we need to call a shopper at Brown Thomas?"

I couldn't afford a shopper. This was just a vetting process and he was being nice because he was a friend of the family. That's all this was.

That's what I kept telling myself so my heart would stop beating so rapidly.

"I'm not going, Mum. He's just doing a favor for Granddad."

Granddad frowned, sitting up in his chair. "Gracie, you're a smart girl, and we both know Jack and his brothers would be lucky to have you in the company. You two may have gotten off on the wrong foot the other night, but once he sees what a hard worker you are, he'll call you in for an interview and hire you on the spot. And there's plenty of room for advancement in the company."

"I don't know," I muttered. I couldn't seriously consider

this. It was a joke. It had to be. That was why Sean probably stopped by. The little bugger wanted to give me shit.

I pulled out my phone, quickly typing in a message to him.

*When were you going to tell me about this job prank? Working for Jack? After I embarrassed myself like that in front of him? Over my dead body.*

"Jack's assistant also tells me there is a furnished flat available, included with the weekly pay," Granddad's voice carried over me.

I looked up from my phone, staring at his raised bushy eyebrows.

This may have been a favor for my Granddad, but what if I really could get the job? I'd have a place to work on freelancing as well and not live with my grandparents. I could maybe save up to get my own place someday.

But first I actually had to get hired for the job before any of that could happen. My phone vibrated in my hand, alerting me I had a message.

Sean: *No jokes here. Just wanting you to come join the Murphy family.*

Sean: *By that I mean work. Don't shag my brother or throw alcohol on him. Please and thank you.*

Me: *Isn't that what your brother's assistant does? Becomes a Murphy? Think he'll propose on the first day as long as I don't spill anything?*

Sean: *You're a pain in the ass, you know that?*

Me: *And you love me for it.*

Sean: *Does this mean you're going through the*

*application process?*

Me: *Is a fully furnished flat really included?*

Sean: *Ah. You can deal with Jack for that I'd say. Just moved out of it and cleaned it myself. Waiting for his new EA: Grace Evans.*

The hairs on the back of my neck stood on end thinking about having to face Jack's scowl every day. But I'd handled him in my childhood and teen years, who's to say I couldn't work with him a few months in the office? It would get me out of my grandparents' house at least, and it could help beef up my resume a bit while I looked for something else.

"Okay. I'll do it. I'll apply," I said, quickly stuffing my phone in my pocket.

What could it hurt? It was a job opportunity. And if it was a real one, and there was a flat coming with it, I could put up with Jack Murphy for a little while.

As long as there was no champagne around.

# Chapter Four

JACK

The look on Grace's face was a mixture of shock and something else. I couldn't put my finger on it. By her wide eyes and slightly parted lips, she probably wished she was anywhere but in front of me.

Was I that much of an arsehole to her? It probably was an accident after all, but I found a smile crossing my lips.

It was fun to banter with her the other night. Maybe Fallon was right; a sit down couldn't hurt. She was the only applicant who got 100 percent on the proofreading portion and every other test.

And teasing her in the interview could be fun. Aileen stood in the open doorway, chewing at her bottom lip.

"Mr. Murphy, Um, Ms. Evans is here for your two o'clock."

I nodded. "I can see that Aileen. I'm sure accounting will be happy to have you back if this goes well with Ms. Evans."

Aileen smirked, muttering something under her breath

before she scampered off and shut the door behind her.

That left just me and Grace, who wore a tight green skirt and a black blouse that was probably supposed to appear professional but instead had me thinking about the curve of her collarbone and how I wanted to run my tongue along her bare flesh.

*What the feck?*

Not only was she mouthwateringly sexy, but the smolder and sass that came with her curvy figure had me thinking about anything other than a chat to discuss the position of my assistant.

"Mr. Murphy, first off, I just want to apologize for the other night. I shouldn't have spilled my drink. Which was totally an accident. I swear." She pressed her hands together, her teeth slightly clenched and bending slightly at the waist.

Normally I would have grumbled at the apology or blown it off. But with her, something kept me going forward.

"Thank you for your honesty, Ms. Evans. I appreciate that. And I accept your apology. Now please, have a seat," I said with a small nod, motioning to the leather chair in front of my desk.

She straightened her shoulders before gingerly sitting as if the chair was on fire.

I wasn't that bad, was I?

"Whatever the reason you're here, I'm glad you are, and I should apologize for my forwardness at the gala."

She blinked hard. Hell, if I were in her seat I would have, too. "You're actually apologizing to me? That's a first."

I cocked an eyebrow. "I'm not sure what you mean."

She narrowed her dark eyes. How did I not notice them before? They were always hidden behind some clunky glasses, but now they were hard not to get lost in.

Feck. Feck. Feck.

This was an interview, not a first date. I had no reason

to be staring at her and wondering if it would go against company conduct to ask if we could move this to the pub. Somewhere less stuffy.

"Look, Jack, I know you probably didn't want me here and you just did this meeting to discuss the position because of my grandfather. I really do need a job and a possible flat of my own for myself and my dog. I may not have experience in this field, but I'm a fast learner. And I promise not to bugger this up."

She let out a low breath and swore. "Shite. Sorry. I didn't mean to use those exact words."

She slammed her fists down on her thighs. "Blast, I did it again."

I admired her cheekiness.

I would have kicked most women out of my office at this point. But not her. I felt like I owed it to Seamus. The old man always had my brothers' and my back, and if he was asking for a favor, I had to at least look into hiring Grace.

Not only were her test scores impressive, her former employer raved that she wished they hadn't downsized and they had kept her.

This woman was fit for the position, that was for sure, but could I stand looking at her outside my office every day? Wondering what would have happened if that drink had never spilled. If I would have stopped playing her little game and just opened my mouth to say I knew who she was. That she looked gorgeous and I wanted to get her alone and see how soon we could get reacquainted.

"Ms. Evans," I said, before standing up and buttoning my suit jacket.

Her gaze trailed from my face down my suit, her neck bobbing with a hard swallow.

"Your CV says you're freelancing which is hard to believe after looking at it. A degree in English literature from the

University of Zurich, student professorship with Fachverein, and even an internship with one of the biggest publishers in Europe that led to a job."

I steepled my fingers together. "But you don't have any experience in this industry. Or this position. Just because I owe your Grandda, doesn't mean I can just hire you without proper protocol, even if you're the most qualified person."

I slowly stepped around the desk until I was right in front of her.

Hell, I really did need to hire her. But I thought I'd at least give her a few moments to ponder this. If she could play with me the other night, I could throw it right back.

"Look, this is a waste of time for both of us. I'll go." She stood up and turned toward the door.

Shite. That wasn't what I expected.

"I don't want you to leave." My words were lower, huskier than I intended.

I leaned back against my desk, crossing my arms over my chest while offering a smile to lighten the mood. "I need a new executive assistant."

"And you think I really can do this job? Even after everything?" Her mouth parted slightly as she took in a sharp breath.

"Aileen wants to go back to working in accounting just as bad as I want someone who can actually handle the job. Someone who is organized and doesn't second-guess everything. A competent human being who can think on her feet, and who isn't afraid to speak up.

"You had no problem playing a little game with me when you knew I didn't recognize you at first. You're smart and personable—that is when you aren't giving me a hard time."

Her cheeks flushed crimson as she looked at her feet instead of me.

Blast, she was cute.

"I'd say you're the right person for the job, even without the experience. I'm the first to admit I can be an arsehole at times. I need someone who knows me. Who can handle this position and whatever else gets thrown at them. Just be careful with the spills."

She shook her head, her brown curls swishing against the silky material of her blouse where her hair fell to her shoulders as she smiled and slowly looked up. "You're never going to let me live that down, are you?"

I couldn't help the grin that spread across my face, my heart beating in a steady rhythm just looking at her. "Eventually I might."

She sighed, started to roll her eyes, but then stopped as if she thought better of it. "I don't have any actual assistant experience, as you know. I've been an assistant editor since I graduated uni, but that was combing through manuscripts. If you're looking for someone to work in your marketing department as an entry-level copyeditor, I'd be more qualified for that."

"You can work your way up. But for now, I'm offering you this position. My assistant. For at least six months, then I can see about you moving up." I pushed off my desk and closed the distance between us.

She looked up at me, a few inches still between us with her in tall black heels. Her lips were slightly parted and her eyes wide.

This wasn't the little girl on her Granddad's farm anymore. This was a sexy, grown woman who smelled like vanilla and coffee. She was real. My heart beat steadily with each breath. What if she said no or walked out that door? I wouldn't chase after a girl, but screwing this up could feck up a whole lot of other things. Like my working relationship with her grandfather.

Or the chance to see her again. Even if it was just at the

office.

"What do you say? Do we have a deal?"

"I'll need to earn twenty percent more than what you have as the starting salary and to move into the furnished flat as soon as possible," she blurted, the feisty courage bubbling in her that had me shaking my head.

"Do you even know what the salary offer is?" I replied.

She smiled. "No, but I'd like twenty percent over. That is if you really do remember who I am, and that like my grandfather, I'd never enter an agreement without a little bargaining."

I nodded firmly, trying not to laugh at her bravado. I held my hand out for her to shake. "Ten percent and you can move in as soon as this interview is over."

She glanced at my outstretched hand then back to my face before holding her palm to me. "Fifteen percent and we have a deal."

Laughing, I took her hand, shaking it. "Welcome to Murphy's Pub, Grace."

• • •

It wasn't more than twenty minutes after the interview that Sean and Connor burst into the office.

"So? Do you have a new assistant?" Connor asked, shutting the door behind him.

"Grace isn't answering my texts," Sean added.

I cracked my neck, signing another document from our Boston office. "Don't you two knock?"

Sean stomped around my desk and whirled my chair toward him with one beefy arm.

"What the hell?" I growled, staring at his wide blue eyes that were focused on the space underneath my desk.

"I thought maybe since she wasn't answering, maybe she

was still here and…doing something."

I straightened, standing and buttoning my jacket. "And if she was?"

A twinge of guilt hit as soon as I said the words. I wasn't that crass to just have her under my desk like that.

Sean glared. "Then I'd have to kick your ass."

I raised an eyebrow, my gut twisting at the words about to come out of my mouth. "Don't tell me after all of these years you finally pulled your head out of your arse and are going to ask Grace out?"

He sighed, shaking his head before running a hand through his beard. "No. It's not like that with us. Besides, I barely have time for anything more than a night with my schedule. Practices have started and rumor has it, New Zealand is looking for a new hooker. Eyes on the prize."

I mentally pumped my fist, trying not to smile knowing that my brother didn't harbor some unrequited love for his best mate.

Not that I had any right. Thanks to what just transpired, she worked for me. There were rules about that sort of thing.

"Is that before or after next spring?" Connor asked, stepping next to Sean and stopping my internal celebration.

Sean raised an eyebrow, then recognition must have dawned on him because he swore under his breath. "Feck."

"Now you two both can't marry Grace, but I'm sure one of you would make a great match," Connor said, clasping Sean's shoulder.

"I get the urgency in us getting married to fulfill the heir clause, but don't you think it's a little rash to assume we'll both go for not only the same girl, but a girl we've known most of our lives?" I asked.

Connor laughed. "You barely paid attention to the bird growing up. You were always busy doing your own thing. I almost didn't recognize her when I saw her recent photos.

But then again, I didn't hit on her at a gala and not know who she was at all."

I frowned. "The glasses and braces are gone and other finer assets have appeared."

I treaded my words carefully, not mentioning how it wasn't just her beautiful arse but the snarky smile that kept me thinking about her long after the gala.

"She's definitely grown up," Sean muttered.

I let out a breath, raking my fingers through my hair. "I'm not going to step in between you and a girl. You two are best mates. Hell, she's a family friend too. I don't want her in that way. She'll be a grand assistant. That's it."

Though even as I said the words out loud, each one was like putting a knife through my chest.

Connor tilted his head to the side, hitching a thumb at each of us. "Is this some sort of Judgement of Solomon thing and you're both trying to take her and I have to offer to cut her in half to see who has the real interest? Or are we just talking about her as an assistant?"

Sean and I both stared at my wide-eyed brother who shrugged. "What? I paid a little bit of attention in Sunday school. She's grand, and I'm not trying to talk about her like a piece of meat, but let's be honest, there's the ticking time bomb of an inheritance clause so we do need to discuss if there's a love interest."

Sean let out a breath, shaking his head before his eyes grew dark. "Jack, I love you as a brother, but you don't have the best track record with women or assistants. I want Grace to take this job because I know she needs it and I know she can handle you. But I don't want to see her get hurt in the process if you're thinking about her as more than that."

My jaw clenched, and it took everything I had not to tell my little brother to piss off. "I have no interest in hurting her. She's just my assistant."

Sean nodded. "Okay. I can accept that. Just be good to her, all right?"

Connor laughed. "I think that's the warning you should be giving her. I'll make sure no one has any champagne around the office."

"Or coffee for that matter. That could be an HR nightmare," Sean added, rocking back on his heels.

"I'm glad you two have so much faith in me," I muttered.

"Hey, what kind of brothers would we be if we didn't give you some shite?" Connor asked, putting his hand on my shoulder.

He was right, but I wouldn't tell him that.

The past few months we'd really started to work together as a team. This last board meeting proved that we had it in us to run this company together.

But if Sean and I didn't find wives soon, our comfortable little roles would quickly be filled by one of the half-dead old men who sat in that boardroom.

There was no bloody way in hell I was going to let that happen.

Now I just had to get Grace off my mind long enough to find a wife. For better or for worse.

# Chapter Five

I applied another coat of lipstick and fluffed my hair one last time in the mirror, staring wide-eyed at my own reflection. "What are you doing, Grace? It's your first day of work. Not a date."

The white blouse and black pencil skirt hugged my curves. At my old job, everyone wore jeans and T-shirts. But this was a corporate office where every man was in a suit and woman in a blazer when I went in for the job interview.

I reluctantly had to have Grandmum help me buy a new outfit for my interview and she added a few more blouses and skirts to my buggy.

I promised I'd pay her back, even after staring at the ridiculous price tags. But Grandmum waved me off as she always did and purchased a bag that had popcorn printed on it and cost more than my weekly salary.

I sighed then glanced around the room that was now mine. The flat was a small studio but it did have a bed, comfortable furniture, and everything I needed in the bathroom and kitchen to live comfortably. I just couldn't get used to it because as soon as my six months were up as Jack's assistant, I'd be out of there and hopefully on to something else.

At twenty-three, I thought I'd have my life together.

I figured that being here, not just in Dublin, but in the flat, was only temporary. But the longer we stayed, the more our lives became ingrained with Grandmum and Granddad's and I couldn't imagine leaving the city.

But, as much as I loved them, a girl also needed her space. Especially when Grandmum didn't understand you couldn't sit on the loo and have a full conversation while someone else was taking a shower.

Maybe working for Jack wasn't my dream job, but it did afford me with a flat, and the ability to clean up without having a conversation about the queen's dogs.

Jane Pawsten whined at my feet, as if she knew she was going to be left alone in a new place until someone came to walk her. I knelt down and picked up the little dog who stared up at me with beady little black eyes.

She groaned as I walked the few steps from the bed to the couch and put her in her crate. She snorted, standing up and turning in a circle until she was facing the other direction and away from me.

"Aw, come on girl. Don't be like that," I cooed. I needed someone to reassure me I wasn't making a mistake by going into this new job today. Even if that someone was a dog.

I frowned, staring at her open cage door and fluffy dog butt. "Would a bully treat make up for it?"

Jane's ears perked and she sat up, turning around with a wagging tail.

"Of course you want the bull penis," I muttered, standing up and walking to the kitchen. I grabbed one of the withered little bones and handed it to the happy dog who now stood at my feet. Out of principle, I wanted to wrinkle my nose at the small gray bones, but Jane loved them.

She ran in a circle then headed to her cage, gnawing the little bone inside as she curled up on her pink cushion.

If she could be content with her new situation, then I could too.

"See you soon, Jane. Wish me luck on my first day of work," I said, locking the cage and grabbing my purse. Mum and Grandmum were coming later in the day to take her out and feed her, so she wouldn't be completely alone and that eased my mind a little bit.

Sometimes I wished my life were as simple as Jane Pawsten's. I'd get fed, taken out to pee, and if I were really distraught, someone would give me a calcified bull penis.

Maybe not that last part.

But I wasn't a dog, and now it was time to face my fate and my first day of work for Jack Murphy.

• • •

I hated being late for anything, so I made sure to be at the office early.

As I strode into the building at quarter till eight, Jack was already sitting in his office with the door open. He wore a white button-down oxford with the sleeves rolled up, showing his well-toned arms. His suit jacket was thrown over the chair.

As if he could feel my eyes on him when I approached, a dimpled grin spread across his face. "Grace, good to see you're early."

He barely looked up from the stack of papers on his desk and my heart beat faster and slower at the same time, willing that smile to be because of my presence.

Blast. I couldn't be attracted to this guy.

He was my boss now. No romantic feelings allowed.

"I thought I'd be the only one here, though," I said, slowly walking into his office.

Those vibrant blue eyes honed in on me.

*Bloody hell.*

*He's gorgeous.*

I may have admired him a few times when we were younger, but I was just another one of Sean's friends. More like furniture rather than an actual girl who deserved his attention.

I mentally chastised myself and curtailed the heat rising within me. I couldn't be thinking like that.

I was a strong, confident woman who didn't need a guy to look at her just to feel better about herself. I didn't need a man at all, certainly. Unless, of course, that man was now my boss and I had to be nice.

His eyes roamed over my blouse and pencil skirt like they had the day before. I swallowed the lump in my throat, trying not to wonder what he was searching for in his stare, and straightened my shoulders, willing myself to stand tall and show him I was all business. Even if the fluttering in my stomach was attempting to say something else, I didn't need the arrogant playboy's attention. Damn him for making these new feelings bubble inside me that were screwing with my head.

"When does Fallon arrive to train me, or will it be Aileen?" I asked, trying not to gaze at the dimple in his right cheek.

"Fallon should be in soon, but until then I can help get you set up." He stood, sauntering toward me. Each step made my heart thump harder.

"Really? The CEO is going to train his assistant?" I furrowed my eyebrows, keeping my voice light.

"Acting CEO or I was until the board decided there would be a hold on that official title until..." His words

50

IRISH ON THE ROCKS

trailed, and he glanced out the window before looking back to me. A crack in his bravado. "Well, until—doesn't matter. Now, come on. Let's at least boot up your computer."

I wanted to ask what this "until" was really about, but before I could even open my mouth, he walked past me and was bent over the desk just outside his office.

Maybe I'd have to ask Granddad what was really going on with Murphy's Pub. But that would have to wait until later.

While his office was dark wood walls and leather seating, the desk and cubicles outside his office were almost sterile. Each polished wooden desk looked like the one next to it. The only thing that made the assistant's area stand out was the fact there was no cube around it, and the back was to a large, gothic-style arched window with the view of the River Liffey.

"I do know how to start a computer," I quipped, making my way toward the work area until I was standing next to him as he clicked a few buttons on the sleek monitor.

"Are you always this much of a smart-ass when people try to help you out?"

"I'm just stating a fact."

He had a mysterious glint in his eyes before his glare went back to the computer. "Here's another fact for you. We have all of our systems password protected. If your system is idle for more than ten minutes, the screen automatically goes back to locked. A pain in the arse, but supposedly it helps with security."

I nodded. "I think most computers have that feature now."

He stopped clicking the screen, and when he looked up, it was as if his dark blue eyes were burning right through me. I didn't know whether to be scared of my new boss or turned on.

"Most people don't talk this much shite to their boss,

especially not on the first day."

I wasn't most people, and I wanted to tell him as much. Then I thought about the flat, my own space that wasn't with my mum and grandparents. The fact that this was the only job offer I had that wasn't hit-or-miss freelancing with demanding authors. If this was going to work, I had to maybe reign in the smart-assery. At least a little bit.

So I shrugged. "Just trying to speed up the process. Letting you know that I really am a fast learner."

He squinted slightly then slowly nodded. "I guess you're right."

"What was that again? I never thought I'd hear Jack Murphy utter those words." I leaned closer, inhaling his manly scent with a hint of mint on his breath. As if he had popped a few peppermints in his mouth before I arrived. That combined with his woodsy cologne had my senses in overdrive.

If I closed my eyes, I could imagine I was in the presence of any other good-smelling man who wasn't my new boss.

He laughed, shaking his head. "Don't let it get to your head. You still have a lot to learn, and Fallon's the only assistant who lasted longer than six months."

"Are you saying that maybe I should propose to Sean and become a Murphy? Is that the way I move up?"

I gasped, covering my mouth after realizing how far I stepped over the line on that one. Little jabs and joking at the gala were one thing. But I never thought of Sean as more than a brother. I would never think of being with a Murphy just to move up in the company. The family meant too much to my grandfather to do that to them. And that whole I-was-never-getting-married thing extended to even my best friend and his hot brothers.

"I'm sorry," I whispered. "I didn't mean to..."

He leaned in, the distance slowly closing between us.

My breath caught in my throat where I was pretty sure my heart also leaped to.

"I know you and Sean are old pals and you like to joke around. Same with you and me. We have a past together that hasn't always been the best, especially after last weekend. But while we're at the office, I'd like to keep this as professional as possible. Okay?" He raised his eyebrows, his eyes so dark they were practically midnight.

I knew it wasn't so much of a question as it was a statement.

"Jack, are you being nice?" The question came from a deep Irish accent and I gasped with a jolt.

I jumped back. But Jack barely moved, looking over the monitor as his middle brother, Connor, breezed in with a tray of steaming foam cups in one hand and the other on his wife's waist.

He grinned like he always did when I saw him, no matter if it was a photo on the internet or when we were kids. He always had the trademark Murphy dimples flashing.

With the beautiful wife next to him, they looked like the perfect pair. Like they belonged on a freaking romance novel.

"You probably need something stronger than a coffee. Maybe after quittin' time, you can add a little something Irish to it," Connor said with a wink once he reached us and handed me a cup.

Now things were starting to make sense. Figured Connor would have a gorgeous wife like her. So the blonde must be Fallon. She was a very lucky girl, even though he was a pain in the arse. At least he was the nicer of Sean's older brothers.

"Thank you, Connor," I said politely.

His smile turned into an all-out grin. "And thank you, Grace, for taking this job with my brother. I promise you; I won't forget who you are, so no need to spill the coffee on me."

Heat crept up my neck. I was going to be forever known

as the girl who spilled drinks, even though it was an accident. Not exactly the impression I wanted to give, but I also didn't expect to be offered a job after that, either.

"That was just an accident. Definitely won't happen again. At least I hope not," I muttered the last part.

"Connor, don't you have somewhere to be so Fallon and Grace can get started on training?" Jack growled.

Connor's happy face faded. Fallon pushed up her red-framed glasses and nodded slowly. It was as if they had an entire conversation just through their eye contact.

These two had only known each other for a few months from what Sean had said, but they were so in sync. A tinge of envy gurgled in my stomach. I'd only seen that in the movies and never had this with another person. Not even my best mates.

But I couldn't concentrate on that. Then I'd start thinking about fairy tales and other things that weren't ever going to happen for me.

"Guess this means you and I are going to go over reports while these two get started," Connor said.

Jack nodded. "Yes."

Neither of the men said another word as they headed to the office, shutting the door behind them.

"I'm Fallon, by the way. The one who emailed you. Connor's wife. Jack's former assistant. All of that." She laughed slightly.

Everything about her was more laidback compared to my starched outfit that felt more like I was a little girl playing dress up. I should have just suggested I pick out my own outfit instead of Grandmum, and gone to a nice vintage shop or boutique for myself.

"I'm Grace." I said, putting my hand out and shaking hers.

"I could tell the instant I walked in and saw Jack's

shoulders squared. I think you scare him and that's something I don't think I've ever seen a woman do."

"Is that a good or bad thing?" I asked, my heart beating faster at the thought.

*Blast, Grace, get a grip.*

She beamed. "I guess we'll see. But first, I'll get you signed into the system, and you can set your passwords."

"Thanks for assuming I know how to use a computer."

She blinked hard. "Please tell me that was sarcasm."

I laughed before nodding. "Yeah. No need to worry about that one."

• • •

The morning went by reasonably quick. Fallon helped me get situated on the company's system and walked me through some of the programs to view Jack's calendar and set up reports.

She was very easy to get along with and had an infectious laugh. I didn't have many friends back in London since I was always working. I figured maybe Dublin was a chance for a new start and perhaps to make some new friends.

When lunchtime rolled around, I thought about asking Fallon to lunch as a thank you for helping me.

Before I could even ask her, though, the phone next to my desk rang.

"Offices of Jack Murphy, this is Grace, how may I help you?"

"Hi Grace, this is Michelle from security. There is a woman here by the name of Elizabeth Walsh who is here to see you. If you could please come down here to meet her."

Every hair on the back of my neck stood on end.

"What is she doing here?" I hissed under my breath, wondering why my mother was at the office instead of walking my dog.

"Pardon?" Michelle asked.

"Nothing. Nothing. I'll be down in a minute. Thank you. Goodbye," I said quickly and hung up the call, looking to the wide-eyed Fallon.

"So my mum decided to stop by, for some unknown reason. You don't mind if I head downstairs to talk to her for a few minutes, do you?" I asked, standing up and grabbing my purse.

Fallon shook her head and picked up her own bag. "No problem. I'll walk you down there."

"Okay. Thanks," I said with a nod.

I probably shouldn't have subjected myself to the embarrassment of my mum showing up at the office. But I wasn't exactly sure how to get back down to the front desk, so I could use all of the help I could get.

Once we got to the main lobby, Fallon's eyebrows shot up then both our eyes trailed to the woman in an empire waist dress and large sunhat, holding a box from a bakery.

"Mum. What an unexpected surprise. Is everything okay?" I asked, trying to keep my tone neutral.

Fallon bit her bottom lip, but I caught the hint of a smile.

Mum narrowed her eyes slightly and tilted her head. "Gracie, dear, it's your first day at the office. I was able to use the key to get into your flat without a problem. After walking and feeding little Janey, I thought you might be hungry and brought some croissants from this little café. Probably not as good as the ones we had in London, but they'll do."

She held the box out to me, but her eyes and body kept pointing toward the closed door behind the giant oval oak desk of the security officers.

"Are you sure everything is all right?" I asked again, wondering if she wanted a tour of the building. With all of the security clearances, there was no way I could do that. And this wasn't just some mom-and-pop shop. This was a large corporation with eight floors and the main level not only housed security, but a museum and one of the first Murphy's Pubs.

Mum waved her wrist. "Don't be silly, darling, especially not in front of your colleagues."

She put her hand out to Fallon. "I'm Elizabeth. Grace's mother."

Fallon stepped closer and shook her hand, her face practically glowing. "It's nice to meet you, ma'am. I'm Fallon Murphy."

Mum's eyes widened. "As in Jack Murphy?"

Fallon laughed. "He's my brother-in-law. I'm married to Connor, the middle Murphy brother."

"Oh. Well, he's a very lucky man, and it's a pleasure to make your acquaintance." Mum used the same too-cheery tone she had when she was trying to schmooze people.

I hated it on any ordinary occasion, but it especially made my blood boil today. Not just because it was my first day of work and she was interrupting, but because I genuinely liked Fallon and didn't need Mum's fakeness interfering.

"Mum, why don't I walk you out? I'm sure you have some work you need to get back to around granddad's house." I squared my shoulders, taking the bakery box with a forced smile.

"Oh, darling, I always have time for my daughter."

There went that voice again.

Sure, we had our moments of getting along. And dare I say even some laughs when we moved from the UK.

But we never were great pals like some mothers and daughters I always sort of envied. What we did was survival. To keep up appearances and not admit that either of us was flat broke, we moved to Dublin to "help out my grandparents." But that was the closest we'd ever come to a bonding moment.

This was the woman who sent me to boarding school as soon as I was out of nappies and shipped me to Granddad's every summer. She had no desire to spend a ton of alone time with me, and we both knew that. Now I needed to get to the bottom of why she was really here.

It took everything I had not to leave claw marks on her arm as I placed my hand near her elbow. "I could use some fresh air. Come on, I'll show you out."

Looking over my shoulder, Fallon gave me a sympathetic nod. "I'll be back in a bit. I hope that's okay."

She nodded. "That's fine. It's about lunchtime anyway. Maybe we can grab a bite and bring some back to your boss, too. Do you think he likes pasty? Do you know what Jack likes, Fallon?"

Fallon bit her lip, her shoulders shaking as if she was trying to hold back a laugh. "I'm not sure."

"I don't know. Maybe I'll ask him when he's done with one of his important meetings," I said, trying to move Mum along.

Even though we were literally at the front doors of the building, it still felt like it took eons to finally get outside and I could take in a deep breath of the stale summer air.

"Darling, you didn't even give me a tour. Should we go back in or head to that charming little pub I saw right around the corner?"

I let go of her arm and slowly took a step back, shaking my head. "What are you really doing here, Mum? You know I can't rightfully give you a tour. This is a big company. There are security clearances."

She opened her mouth with an angry scowl on her face. "Grace Louise, I can't believe you're talking to your mum like this."

"Mum...really."

She stuttered out a breath before clearing her throat

and put her hand on her chest. "I was just having tea with Grandfather and Grandmother when your grandfather happened to mention an heir clause in the late Mr. Murphy's will."

"What does that have to do with anything? Why would that make you show up here with baked goods?" I huffed, gripping tightly onto the little pink box.

She glanced at the empty pavement before stepping closer and lowering her voice. "What that means is that the will states each son has to be married to earn their stake in the company. If all three boys aren't married within a year, their shares of Murphy's Pub will go to the highest bidder on the board."

I shook my head, this blast of information swimming in my brain. Why hadn't Sean told me about this?

Was she telling the truth? And if so, what did this mean for the boys and the company?

"That sounds archaic and not like something that would go in a modern will," I grumbled.

Mum nodded, a small quirk of her lips into a half-sneer, half grin. "But it is."

"And what about it? If you're saying I should marry Sean, you're out of your mind as he's one of my oldest friends. And if it's about Jack, just don't even go there. I am just doing this job as a favor to Sean and Granddad."

How could she even think I would after everything she and Father went through?

Her lips turned upward into a sinister smile, like a cartoon villain. "I'm not saying marry him at all. But you do have your womanly charms, and if he happened to fall for you, that would keep him from marrying anyone else. Thus, leaving a share of the company open to Grandfather."

My head throbbed with this new information. No way in hell I'd do any kind of crazy scheme Mum conjured up, but that didn't stop me from thinking about it. If Granddad bought the company, it would secure me a job, and of course whatever inheritance Mum could get. Then maybe she'd finally get back on her feet and even head back to London.

But as the thought crossed my head, it quickly floated away. I would never do that to the brothers, no matter how much it could set up my family. And that was the twinge of guilt that had now buried itself deep in my chest.

"This is ridiculous. You do know that, right?" I narrowed my eyes.

Her shoulders slumped. "Do with it what you will, but know that this is a way to secure all of our futures. Your grandparents won't be around forever. They have some money put away, but a stake in the company could really change all of our lives."

I sucked in a deep breath. Her words rang true, no matter how malicious they were. I just couldn't think like that, even if it was an enticing thought. I had to go back inside. I couldn't think about this. Not now. Not ever.

"I need to get back to work, Mum. I'll see you for tea on Sunday?"

She blinked rapidly before straightening her dress and nodding. "I'll see you Sunday. Maybe even invite Jack, too. I'm sure Grandfather and Grandmother would love to see him."

I shook my head, knowing there was no way I would ever bring Jack to anything with the family. Especially not after this little conversation Mum and I just had. Besides, it's not like we were anything other than co-workers or old family friends.

And that's all we'd ever be.

"I'll be sure not to ask him."

# Chapter Six

JACK

For years, I wanted my da's position as CEO, and now that Connor was taking over the responsibilities of CFO, things were much easier. During the call with some of the franchise investors in America, Connor was the one who had to prepare the points and would eventually write up something his assistant would send out.

I dreaded that moment in every single meeting, thinking how the hell I was going to take everything we just discussed in a two-hour phone call and somehow make everyone happy with a one-paragraph memo.

Luckily Fallon was pretty quick on her heels and had gotten everything sent out in a timely manner. No other assistant had worked like her. But Grace, I had a feeling, would be a close second.

I wasn't lying when I said her CV was impressive. How a woman with her grades, internship, and school experience wasn't working with some big publisher was beyond me.

Whoever had interviewed her before me didn't know what they were missing.

I never thought the little punk girl with glaring brown eyes would be the one who would make me shudder and beam all at the same time. She was maddening and had always been good at getting under my skin. Even as a little girl who would hide rocks in my shoes right before I went to leave the house. She and Sean would each put the blame on each other, but that sassy little smirk of hers always gave it away.

Just like it did now.

Like it should have the night of the gala.

She may have acted like she didn't want this position in the company, and tried to glare, but when the words actually reached her lips there was that little hint of something more. But I could never tell if it was an impending doom sort of look, or a you're-not-bad-for-an-arsehole kind of thing.

I was supposed to be finding a wife, not thinking about a girl from the past whom I wasn't even sure I liked as anything more than a friend of the family.

Connor was right that we couldn't talk about her like she was a piece of meat to fight over. She was just supposed to be an assistant. Not a love interest.

That's what I had to keep telling myself and ignore the rush that rattled my body every time I saw that smile of hers.

"I don't know how you did this shite for so long. There has to be an easier way." Connor shook his head, going through the pages of scribbles on the desk.

"Hey, if you've got one, I'm all ears," I said, putting my palms out.

He shook his head, looking up from his papers. "Maybe that new assistant of yours has an idea. Heard she was an assistant editor at some publishing house. They know how to tighten and cut what's needed."

I narrowed my eyes, unsure what kind he was trying to

get at. "She was an assistant editor. Now she's my assistant, and I don't think editing romance novels works the same way as procedures in a company."

He shrugged, picking up the papers and going toward the door. "Yeah, but it couldn't hurt."

Then he opened the door before I could respond.

Instead of the two women huddled over the computer, Fallon sat in the seat outside of my office.

It was past lunchtime, but surely Grace would have sent a note if she was leaving.

Or quitting.

My pulse quickened, my eyes widening as I stalked toward the door, looking at the empty chair then to Fallon. "Where is Grace?"

She blinked, looking up from the computer. "Uh, she was just walking her mom out. She brought some croissants which she pronounced all French-like."

I listened to about half of Fallon's rambling but focused on my still racing heartbeat.

"Sure she didn't try to escape? Because that's a pretty good excuse," Connor said with a wink before he turned toward me.

"Already have the new girl running for the hills? And I thought she'd be able to handle you." He laughed.

I knew she probably hadn't already gone through the process of quitting, but what would I do if she left? Would that give me the green light to proceed with something more outside the office?

But then again, I did need an assistant. The turmoil played over and over in my head.

Relief finally washed over me when Grace's heels clicked on the wooden floor as she crossed to the desk and dropped a bakery box on the corner as if it were just another piece of office furniture.

"Sorry. Just had to slip out for a minute. But I'm back now if you need me to do anything. Oh, and there are croissants. Mum brought them as a first-day-of-work thing. I know, weird, but she means well," Grace said, her voice on the edge of frazzled.

"You can take lunch if you need to. Your mam coming to visit doesn't count, so you can have the extra time." I nodded, trying to ignore the new pang in my chest.

"It's fine. I can work through it. I have a lot to catch up on. I'll finish these forms now, so I won't have to worry about it later," she said quickly, going to her chair.

Connor opened the pink box on the desk, then closed it before smiling at his wife. "I need more than bread. I think we should head for a bite before I try to tackle my own work."

Fallon tilted her head slightly, and he nodded in return before her mouth formed a perfect O, and she stood. "Yeah. I'll be back soon, Grace, and we can go over the system again."

Grace nodded at the blonde who now scurried around the desk, grasping onto Connor's outstretched hand. "Okay."

As soon as the couple was out of earshot, I leaned on Grace's desk, opening the small box for myself.

I wasn't much for croissants or really any kind of pastry. But the buttery smell wafted from the box and my stomach rumbled.

I couldn't remember the last time I ate. Which was a regular occurrence, with a hurried cup of coffee in the morning. But just because I was too busy to think about a lunch break, didn't mean my new assistant had to suffer as well.

"Why don't you take a break?" I asked.

"What? No. I'm fine." She waved her hand, but her eyes shifting to the box said something else.

"I know that look. This is exactly what you need."

She shook her head. "It's fine really."

"It's me telling you that I know you've been working your arse off half the day and probably forgot to eat. So we're going to sit here and eat something."

Slowly I circled her desk and took the seat next to her. I tried to ignore that our bodies were only a few inches apart and the need to reach out and brush my fingers along her skin was growing more and more urgent. I had to clamp these feelings down, and fast.

"You're seriously crazy if you think I'm going to sit here and stuff my face. I'll just grab something later. Don't worry about me," she quipped, her eyes on the computer.

I grabbed the box of croissants, taking one flaky pastry out, then plopping it on her desk.

"What the bloody hell?" She snapped, scooting back and brushing crumbs off her skirt.

Her eyes widened as she looked up at me. "Shite. I didn't mean to burst like that. But this is a new skirt and…"

She sighed. "Bollocks, I need to learn to control my mouth. This isn't going to HR is it?"

I licked m lips, grabbing a pastry for myself out of the box. "And what would they do, exactly? Tell me not to look out for the well-being of my new assistant? That maybe I need better aim when scooting the food across the table, so I don't drop crumbs all over you?"

She blinked hard and groaned. "You don't have to be nice to me, you know."

"I think I do. I'm just trying to help you out. So, one small bite of the pasty and I'll be out of your hair." I couldn't help the grin spreading across my face.

"If I take a small bite can we never speak of this or the gala again? Call it tit for tat?" she asked, clearing her throat.

"Maybe." I took a small nibble of the croissant, trying not to focus on the curve of her red lips when she smirked.

She grabbed the bread from her keyboard, taking a large bite, swallowing hard, then setting the rest of it down. "There, we even?"

"I guess it's a start." I stood up, circling to the front of her desk.

"You didn't need to do that you know. The food or ignoring my incompetence."

"You aren't incompetent and we both know that. And really, you do need to eat. Can't have a good assistant ignoring her lunch hour."

She looked down at her computer.

"I do eat. If you can't tell by these," she muttered, putting her hands on those curvy hips I was just thinking about. I had to mentally shake my head to ignore the warm thrill blazing through me at the thought of my hands there instead of hers.

"I work from sunup to sundown and sometimes forget to have a snack here and there or cheese with my nightly whiskey. If it wasn't for Fallon making sure she brought in lunch or getting an afternoon snack every day, I would have probably passed out on my desk multiple times."

She shook her head, but still didn't meet my gaze. "I'm not going to bring you coffee and food at your beck and call. I mean I could if that's what you really want, but probably not the best use of my time."

"I didn't say you had to. But if you need to take a break, take it. There's no shame in taking care of yourself. And if you feel like bringing something back, I'm always grateful when someone reminds me to eat."

She narrowed her eyes. "You're not going to tell me about a company gym pass now, too, are you?"

I shook my head, instantly taken back. "What? No. I mean, we do have discounts at local gyms if you wanted to go to one. Not that I'm saying you need it."

Feck. What was this woman doing to me that I was

rambling like Fallon?

I didn't want to be the creepy boss, so instead I met her gaze. "I should get back to work and let you finish your training."

She nodded. "Yeah. Probably."

The conversation should have been over, but I found myself lingering and absently tapped on the wood surface underneath my palms. "When you're done with lunch and your HR paperwork, we should talk about your editing experience and how it can help with some procedures in the company. I'll make sure to send you an detailed email with some instances and things I think could be improved on. Then you can look over them and have some notes before tomorrow."

She widened her eyes with a blush pinching her cheeks. "I don't think what I did…or do…or…"

I couldn't help the laugh that escaped my lips. She always tried to make herself out to be put together, and when she got flustered there was something absolutely adorable about it. "Don't worry. I'm not penning a novel I want you to help me get published in there. I just need some help possibly changing up some procedures to make things easier for all of us."

I finally stood upright and buttoned my suit coat. "Put it on your calendar. Meeting tomorrow at half past nine. I'll bring breakfast. Or maybe we can even meet up at a café down the street."

"This sounds like a date instead of a business discussion with a café and breakfast. You know HR probably wouldn't like that." She may have said the words, but I had a feeling the coy little quirk of her lips meant something else.

"Then I guess it's a meeting and you're getting the coffee." I nodded and headed to my office, closing the door before she could protest.

...

Grace was always prompt.

My smile broadened when I approached the café near Murphy's Pub headquarters. She sat at a little bistro table with two steaming coffee cups and trays of pastries in front of her.

Instead of the starched blouse and stiff skirt, she wore a flowy green dress with a silk sweater. She looked more casual than I'd seen her, and somehow more relaxed than the girl who had been in my office the day before. Something about the dress with her hair down in soft curls made me think about what the woman was like when she did let loose.

Now it was just the two of us, outside the office, and I had to mentally keep myself from saying anything to make me look like a gobshite.

"So you did get my coffee?" I asked, taking the seat across from her.

She barely looked at me, but a slight smile crossed her lips. "Don't get too used to it. I figured I couldn't order just one cup and not bring one for you, too."

"Noted. But I think this means you might kind of like me."

I grabbed one of the cups and nodded curtly.

She shook her head, but a smile reached the corners of her lips. "You're okay. But I'm hoping you'll hear me out with these ideas I have."

I blinked. "I'm all ears."

She sighed. "You know my experience is limited to publishing so I don't know how much this will actually help."

She opened a leather portfolio, spreading out papers covered in excel spreadsheets and graphs.

I leaned forward and picked up one of the sheets with my free hand. "Did you prepare all of this just for our meeting?"

Briefly I looked over the sheet, glancing at the brightly color-coded categories and percentages.

"I did a little extra research on the company, after reading through your notes in the email. I wanted to show how one process would correlate to some others," she quipped and sat up straighter. It was evident in her wide eyes that she was proud of her work yet feared rejection.

I nodded. "If you were going to work late, I'd prefer you stay at the office to do it so we can make sure that goes on your timecard. But I will say, this is impressive. Your chart here about how much of my time is spent in meetings that could be forwarded in an email makes me re-think what I've been doing all day. Do I really spend that much time in a conference room?"

She nodded slightly, chewing on her bottom lip. "I hope you don't mind. I did some back digging in your calendar so I could check out some of your meetings and the notes."

"I see that. You really are making me think I need to streamline this process."

She fiddled with the collar of her dress, but didn't respond. Instead, she leaned over the table.

The buttons of her dress pulled at her chest, giving me a view of the lacy black bra peeking through the material

She was talking about numbers and different processes. I had to stop thinking about how beautiful those brown eyes of hers were, but once I started, I couldn't stop.

Feck, what had gotten into me?

Even if there was a physical attraction, I was pretty sure the woman hated me. The old me, at least. The cocky sonofabitch from school. But I was different now, I'd like to think. But it didn't matter. I needed to be looking for a wife, not just someone I could have some fun with. Grace was a family friend and even trying something, could lead to a disaster if it didn't work out. Not to mention Sean's rage that could follow if I hurt his best mate.

"I've got to take this," Grace muttered, knocking me out of my trance.

I didn't even notice her phone was buzzing until she sat down and with a grimace, put the device to her ear.

"Mum, I told you I was in a meeting," she hissed. "Sorry to be short, but…"

Her mum seemed like a nice enough woman. I didn't know much about her, as she wasn't ever around her grandparents' place growing up. But anytime her Mum was mentioned, Grace's face soured. Especially now as she spoke with her.

"Blast," Grace muttered. "Okay. I'll be right there."

She hung up and tossed her phone into her purse.

"Everything okay?" I asked, raising an eyebrow.

She sighed. "I'm sorry to do this, but I'm going to have to take an early lunch, or morning break, or whatever this would be considered. I had to drop my dog off with my mum since she disturbed the neighbors at my flat, barking all day. But while she was out in the garden with Grandmum she got into some plants she shouldn't have and has been getting sick all over the house. I need to meet Mum at the vet."

I'd never had a woman need an escape call or an excuse to leave breakfast with me.

Especially since this was a business meeting and not a date.

Feck. What the hell was going through my head? This was Grace, not a woman I was trying to woo. And if she really was having a dilemma with her pup, no need to be an arsehole about it.

"Your dog?"

She stood up, frowning. "Yes, my dog, Jane Pawsten. She doesn't like to be left alone or ignored for a few minutes or she starts getting into everything."

I opened my mouth and closed it again, shaking my head. There was no easy way to respond to that.

I'd never had a pet myself and never actually understood the grand attachment to them, but the worried look in her eyes and shaking of her hands said this was more than just an excuse. She was really worried.

"I'm sorry again. I have to call a cab and get to the vet in Ballsbridge."

I stood up, straightening my jacket before pulling out my wallet and placing a few notes on the table. If she was this worried, there was no way in hell I was going to let her go alone.

"No need to call a cab. I'll drive you."

She furrowed her brow, shaking her head fiercely. "You don't have to do that. I'm sure you need to get to work."

I smiled, trying to reassure her I really did want to help. "My assistant blocked off an hour and a half on my calendar, so I have some time. Besides, I care about families, even the four-legged kind. I wouldn't want anything to happen to your little Jane Clawsten."

"Pawsten... Like Austen but with a paw in front." She put her hands up, still fidgeting from foot to foot. "Wait. Why am I explaining this to you?"

I took a step closer, so we were only a few inches apart. She looked up at me with those caramel eyes and I saw the tears brimming in them.

I swallowed hard. If something did happen to her dog and she was this attached, would she be able to afford the treatment? She only started working and I didn't know anything about a savings or if Seamus was pitching in.

"Because I'm the one who is going to take you to save your dog," I blurted before I could take it back.

"I'm really sorry about this," she said with a sigh and stepped back.

I nodded and put my arm out, leading Grace toward my car. "No need to apologize. I understand."

I wanted to wrap her in my arms and reassure her that everything was going to be okay. But I actually didn't know if it would be. Or what kind of condition she'd find her pet in. I just knew that she would need someone there with her and I wasn't going to leave her.

She laughed. "I just hope she's okay."

I nodded, worry settling in me, watching this girl's face fall, but I smiled, figuring it was the least I could do. "Let's go save Jane Pawsten."

. . .

Traffic was light on the seven-kilometer drive to Ballsbridge.

The little white building stood out amongst the brick homes and bushes lining the cobblestone street. Not to mention that if my car's GPS hadn't told me we had arrived at our destination, I would have spotted the giant dog murals in the windows from a few meters away.

As soon as we parked the car, Grace bolted for the front door, running faster than I'd ever seen a woman in very high heels go.

Parking my car, I quickly followed her into the small, sterile lobby where three people sat on white plastic chairs. Seamus's wife in her feathered hat, and the other woman must be Grace's mum. She was the one who opened her mouth to speak but was interrupted as Grace pushed a little bell on the front desk repeatedly.

Finally, a woman in white scrubs entered from the back and approached the large wooden desk with a tired expression of sullen eyes and lips in a straight line. "Hello, how can I help you?"

"Yes. I'm here for my dog Jane Pawsten-Evans. Is she

okay?"

I'd seen the nervous and the mischievous woman, but this was an entirely different Grace. Her hands shaky, shoulders slumped, and her eyes wide and wild.

I wished there was something more to do than just stand there.

But I was afraid if I even touched her she'd scurry away, thinking it wasn't just for comfort.

The woman in scrubs nodded, turning to her computer and typing a few things before looking back to Grace. "Ah yes, the little Brussels Griffon. For how sick she was, you'd think she'd lose some of the energy."

Grace laughed slightly but chewed on her bottom lip as she leaned on the counter.

Slowly I stepped forward and put my hand on her lower back. Instead of swatting me away, she leaned into my side. My mouth grew dry with a new warmth spreading through me, trying to hold back whatever was blooming inside of me.

Not the time to think about how she felt pressed up against me or how damn good her floral shampoo smelled. As soon as the back door opened, Grace pushed forward, out of my grasp and her whole face lit up.

"Janey!"

I don't know what I expected, maybe something more meaty than the little tiny furball with an underbite who squirmed in the man's arms that was holding her.

"Is that tiny Chewbacca thing Jane Pawsten?" I asked, pointing at the snorting dog.

I tried to keep the shock out of my voice, but I expected a lethargic beast to come limping out. Not this little thing.

And yet I found myself laughing at the little dog.

"Jane does not look like Chewbacca," Grace said with a half scowl as she took the little thing gently in her arms.

The little dog barely covered her arms as she cuddled her

close, scratching behind the little furball's ears.

I moved closer, taking the dog's tiny paw in my hand. "Nice to meet you, girl. I'm Jack Murphy."

The dog squirmed and yapped, her whole body moving with each little noise.

"You wouldn't believe that just an hour ago she was half asleep, coughing up big mounds of weeds on the carpet. Seamus stepped in one and you should have heard the words he started bellowing," Grace's Grandmum said, shuffling next to Grace, her eyes lighting up under the brim of her large hat.

"Mum, no need to talk about those type of things in front of company," Grace's mum said turning toward me with a an appreciative smirk that wasn't appropriate for the situation.

Grace shuddered, keeping her eyes on the dog, but constantly glancing at the papers and listening to the woman in scrubs describe the aftercare for her dog.

I looked over her shoulder, seeing the amount and what care the dog went through. It seemed ridiculous, but then I remembered all of the bills that it seemed like were still coming in for Da's hospital stay.

For anyone else it would have probably come close to bankrupting them. We were just lucky we could pay. I was sure not everyone else was. And to not be able to pay for your family's care, feck, that really got me.

Maybe Da did pass in the end, but we did everything to make him comfortable and keep him with us a little longer. The same I was sure Grace would do for her family, even if it was just her dog.

"Mr. Murphy, I wasn't expecting you to come with Gracie, but I do appreciate it. She does love that dog," Grace's mum said, adjusting the pearls around her neck and forcing me to turn my attention to her.

"I'm glad I could be here for her," I said softly, glancing

down at the little dog cuddled in Grace's arms.

"You know, since we're out anyway, maybe we can stop and get some tea. I do know there's a little café around the corner from here. That is, if you and Grace aren't too busy," Grace's mum said with a sickly-sweet smile.

Grace finished signing the last piece of paper then pulled out her pocketbook, cringing with each movement. "Mum, we're not here for tea. Janey should be okay now after we give her this medicine and I'll settle her down in her crate. I'll be back as soon as I can after work and give the maids extra instructions for tomorrow," Grace replied quickly. She glared at the older woman who glared right back.

I put my hand over Grace's where she held her pocketbook, a new sense of urgency coursing through me. "Don't worry about work today. Or about this bill."

She blinked hard. "I can't take the day off. It's only my second day. And the bill? Jack you can't…"

Before she could protest anymore I pulled my wallet out of my back pocket and placed a credit card on the sheets of paper. Then I slid the items toward the woman behind the counter. "Make sure all future bills go on this card as well."

"Jack…you don't need to do this. Really."

Grace glanced back at her grandfather who was slowly approaching the counter.

"Jack, I assure you that we can handle this," Seamus said with a shaky voice.

Grace shook her head. "No. Neither of you need to. It's fine. It'll go on this credit card and I can pay it off when I get my first paycheck. It'll be fine."

I mentally calculated what her first paycheck would be in my head. Sure, it would possibly be enough to pay for the dog's bill, but what else? What about follow-up care? Or hell, even food for Grace and the dog.

No way I was letting her go without.

I looked at the little dog instead of the owner who was trying to fight me on paying when I knew she didn't have the money for it. Jane Pawsten stared at me then my hand before sticking her wet nose on my fingertip and snorting.

I didn't know what to make of that until she licked my hand then pawed at my knuckles until I scratched behind her ears.

"I think Jane might be saying thank you," Grace said softly.

My gaze lifted to hers. The once fiery glare had now softened to a warm peek that made a low boil stir inside of me.

Before I could react, the little dog jumped out of her arms and was at my feet. She pawed and looked up at me with large, dark eyes.

"Jane," she gasped, narrowing her eyes at the dog.

The dog looked over her shoulder and yapped then stared back at me.

I smirked, kneeling down and scratching the dog behind her ears.

"She's not usually like this, I swear," Grace sputtered. "Must be the medication."

"I have a way with women."

She zeroed in on Jane who had now curled on the floor, eyelids fluttering.

"I can take her if she's bothering you, probably shedding on your trousers," she offered instead of the quick comeback I was expecting.

I shook my head. "She's fine. From the way you talked about her, I expected some ferocious beast."

She knelt down beside me, running her hand over the dog's fur. "She can be. You just have to know how to handle her."

I met Grace's gaze and wasn't sure if we were talking

about her or the dog anymore. But whatever it was, some unspoken thing passed between us. Something I hadn't felt in a long time but was now making me rethink the girl squatting next to me. And I hope by the small smile, she was thinking the same.

"Are you sure you two don't want to stop for some tea? I'm sure Seamus would love to catch up with you, as well, Jack," Grace's mam's words interrupted us.

Grace sighed, standing up with the little dog back in her arms. "I wish we could, Mum. But really, Jack has a meeting and I need to get back to work, as well. Do you think you'll be able to take care of Janey? If not—I mean…"

I took my credit card back from the woman behind the counter then handed a little bag of prescriptions to Grace. I needed to try and keep this all business between us, but I wasn't an animal and wouldn't make a worker come back with a sick family member. Even if the family member was a dog.

"Really, you can go home with the dog. Or even bring her into the office."

Her eyebrows lifted so high I swore they disappeared into her hairline. "Bring the dog? Wouldn't that be against some building codes?"

I shrugged. "It's my family's building so technically I make the rules. And she can stay in my office. I can call Connor right now and see if he can pick up a dog bed or whatever other necessities we need."

Before I could pull out my phone, Grace furiously shook her head. "As nice as that sounds, I can't inconvenience you like that. You've already done more than enough and I don't know how I'm ever going to be able to repay you."

"I've got a few ideas," Grace's Grandmum said with a laugh, wiggling her eyebrows.

"Mum," Grace's mum chastised.

"At least let me give you a ride home with the dog. Then you can keep an eye on her."

Grace chewed on her bottom lip for a second. "I can't make you do that, either. I know how important your ten-thirty meeting is."

"I promise you we'll text as soon as we get home and I'll send pictures the rest of the day. I can even bring her by the office if she feels up to it," Grace's mum said, putting her hand on her daughter's shoulder, who I swore slightly shuddered in response.

Grace looked between me and her mum before she finally sighed. "Okay. But only because I do need to get back to work. But please, please call me as soon as you get home, okay?"

Her mum nodded, taking the sleeping dog who snorted as she adjusted herself again.

My gaze followed Grace's shaking hands that stilled at her sides once the dog was out of her arms and she went to give her mother more instructions. And just like that, the woman with the soft voice was gone, and back was my nervous assistant.

Would I get to see the woman who softened at my touch again?

And if I did, how the hell was I going to be able to resist her?

# Chapter Seven

It had been a little over a week since we went to the vet with Jane.

Jack had even sent a care package to the flat of gourmet dog bones and food.

No man, hell, no person had ever done something like that for my dog.

And while at the office, I was supposed to focus on finishing some HR paperwork before Fallon came into work, but my thoughts kept drifting to him.

He'd always been brooding, almost beastly. The only time he had ever smiled was when he was flirting or expecting something. Watching him melt for Jane Pawsten made every part of me acutely aware of the man before me. I had to count my breaths as I took them, so I didn't let out a sigh watching him pet the little furball's ears. And when he offered to have her come to the office without a second thought? It took everything in me not to embrace him right there.

But I couldn't let my boss's reaction to my dog cloud my judgment. This was a job, and he was the arsehole I'd grown up with. Not to mention, said arsehole was also my best mate's brother.

Just because he had a soft spot for dogs didn't change any of that.

The roll of the chair against the wooden floor signaled that Fallon was about to take the seat next to me. "Hey, Grace? Whoa…are you okay?"

I looked up from my computer where I had been staring at the same page for at least half an hour.

"What? Do I have something on my face?" I asked, wiping at my mouth. I hadn't eaten anything since I wolfed down a little bit of toast and coffee as I ran out the door of my grandparents' place. I'd been dropping Jane Pawsten off in the morning, then hauling arse back downtown to make it into work. Sometimes in between there I'd grab a coffee or something at a café if I had time. Or spare change I found in the couch cushions.

Fallon took her seat with a huge grin and I tried to focus on her instead of my imagination. "You can't even wipe that blush off your cheeks. Something tells me things must be going pretty well with you and this job. Or is this about you and Jack? I've seen you two laughing on more than one occasion when he passes by your desk. I don't think he ever laughed when Aileen was his assistant, nor I for that matter. You must be doing something right."

I shook my head, mentally scolding myself. Blast. I needed to stop thinking about Jack so often. The funny moments that had us both laughing and the other ones that I wouldn't reveal out loud. "No, no. Just amusing wording in these HR forms."

She raised an eyebrow. "There is absolutely nothing remotely comical in those forms."

"I'll have you know this passage about..." I looked at the screen, reading the first line that popped up, "'precatory and concluding activities will constitute compensable hours...' Okay, blast, that isn't funny at all."

"I knew it. You act pissed off at him all the time, but you still took this job and by the way you two look at each other..."

"You're doing that rambly thing again," I muttered, trying to be nice but wanted to know where she was going with her statement.

She shook her head slowly. "What I mean to say is, I guess it's just good to see that you're happy here. Not many assistants walk out of here with anything other than a groan and a name for Jack that I won't repeat out loud."

"I'm just happy to have this job." I said.

She sighed, rubbing her hands down her legs. "Look, it's probably not my place to say, but I'd kind of consider us friends. Maybe I'm overstepping."

She paused and tilted her head slightly.

I nodded slowly. "Yes to friends."

She let out a deep breath, running her palms along the hem of her dress. "Well, as a friend, I should tell you that Jack usually isn't this nice to his assistants. Or invites them to breakfast."

I didn't tell her about our visit to the vet that interrupted our meeting, though she may have noticed I was glancing at my phone a lot more often. I made sure to check in with my mum and make sure Jane stayed out of the plants.

"It was a meeting. It's a job. I did what he told me to do."

He made it seem more like breakfast with a friend, even complimenting me then helping with Jane, which was more than I could have asked from anyone. Ever.

But I couldn't let that cloud my judgement and get soft for the guy.

Even if him getting soft for my Janey was the very thing

that kept melting my heart.

Damn him and being sweet to my dog.

"I'm just saying, it's nice to see Jack and you are getting along. Whether it's work or something else."

I was aching to talk to someone about what my mother had said. To have someone else dissect what the bloody hell was going on. Was the marriage contract real? If it was, was that why Jack was talking and being so nice to me? And why hadn't Sean told me about it?

Who would know better than someone who was married to a Murphy?

"I'm not looking for a relationship. I'm just trying to get settled in Dublin," I muttered, still trying not to think about his piercing blue eyes and the way I wanted more than just his gaze on me.

Fallon shrugged. "Okay."

We were silent for a few more beats before she smiled and turned toward me again. "Hey, Connor has a meeting at five, so how about joining me for dinner after work at the Murphy's downstairs?"

I cleared my throat. "The pub? I thought that was just used as part of the museum not an actual, still-in-operation pub."

"Well, it's the first Murphy's Pub location that they keep open next door to the museum on the first floor. I mean I think technically it's the second location since I heard the first location was in the basement of a funeral home or something."

I widened my eyes and Fallon waved her hands in front of her.

"If you'd rather have something fancier I'm sure I can look up a British-type restaurant for you," she stammered.

I shook my head. "No, no. I didn't even know that was a real working pub and thought you might be sick of that type of fare after working here."

She laughed. "One would think, but I guess all those years of undergrad then my master's conditioned me to live off beer and fries, or chips as you call them. And it'll be on Murphy's tab so if you really want to grind Jack's gears, order whatever you want."

I laughed, liking Fallon's quick wit. And it would be nice not to have to sit alone in the flat, eating jam and crackers for dinner. Maybe I could even bring something back for Jane and check on her real quick before dinner. "Okay let me just message my mum to make sure my dog is okay then I should be good to go."

"Great."

. . .

After a phone call to my mum, and a long talk with the maid about Jane and her medication, I finally headed downstairs with Fallon for dinner.

Strolling into the pub, we made a beeline for the wooden bar and sat down on one of the few empty stools. It may have been a weeknight, but that didn't stop almost every booth and seat from holding a patron with a pint.

"What'll it be, girls?" the beefcake male bartender asked us.

"A pint of Guinness for me," Fallon replied.

"White wine, please," I answered. I didn't plan on having a drink, but since Fallon ordered, I figured I would, too. I just couldn't take the dark beer everyone here drank.

Even though other people were waiting, the bartender poured our drinks, setting them in front of us. The Irish were known for their beer and whiskey and definitely not this watered-down stuff they called wine. But I drank anyway, trying to forget about my moment with Jack at the vet.

Why was he getting to me like this?

If it was true what Mum said about the clause in the will, he needed a wife for the company. Not a girl with dog problems and commitment issues.

Fallon plucked a menu from the condiment caddy, handing me the worn laminated paper. "I think I have this thing memorized, but you probably need a minute."

Thankful for the break in my thoughts, I glanced over the old English text, thinking I should go for the farmhouse salad, but it was hard to turn down a good fish and chips.

After Fallon and I ordered the same thing, she turned to me, looking over her pint. "Now that we're away from the office, I have to bring it up. The history with you and Jack? I'm really curious about it."

"Bloody hell," I muttered, taking a big swig of my drink. I was going to need something a lot stronger if I was going to talk about my childhood.

Not that any of it was terrible. I was just like any other kid at boarding school with parents who shipped her off whenever they could. But my history with Jack was something even I had trouble putting into words.

She raised an eyebrow. "That bad?"

I shook my head. "Not bad, per say, but we were two different people."

I took another gulp of my drink. "I've known him since I was just a wee girl. Sean and I became fast friends, but Jack was a different story. He was always the brooding, popular heartthrob the girls fawned over. I was invisible. The punk girl who would rather read or listen to music with Sean than go to a sporting event. Hell, he didn't even recognize me at first at the gala, and before I knew it, you're emailing me to apply for a job and now here we are."

She smirked. "Obviously you made an impression on him. From one former invisible girl to another, I can say that the Murphy men do like women who know what they want and go for it. Some call us headstrong or bitchy. Take your pick."

"I think my father said the same thing about my mother during their divorce battles. Well the latter," I muttered.

"Shit. Sorry. My parents have called each other all sorts of names. Still don't know why they're together, actually. Probably too cheap for a divorce." Fallon shrugged, but there was something else that said a whole other story behind her gaze.

But I wasn't going to get into that. Just as much as I was sure she didn't want to hear about how my parents' marriage and divorce made me think matrimony and love were bollocks.

I took a drink of my wine then decided to try and put the topic back to her and my curiosity was piqued about how her and Connor actually did get together.

"I didn't think either of us would be a Murphy boys' type, no offense, and not that I'm interested either," I said quickly, setting my glass down, which was soon filled again by the bartender.

"Guys may pretend or even think they want the easy girls who throw themselves at them. But when it comes down to it, they all want someone who will challenge them."

Her gaze trailed across the bar and then her entire face lit up. "Like for instance, right now, with Jack's current date who is boring the hell out of him."

My breath caught in my throat as I gasped involuntarily, following Fallon's eyes to a small table where Jack was seated with a redhead across from him.

Fallon was right. I may not have interacted with Jack much these past few years, but I knew the tapping of his fingers and the constant glances at his phone were never a good sign.

Probably the only reason he was still sitting across from the woman was because he'd do anything to get the CEO title. To keep Murphy's Pub. That made a twinge of guilt hit hard in my gut.

He may have been a wanker at times, but he really did care about his family and friends. He would do what he could for them. Including boring dates and paying for his assistant's dog's medical bills.

"I think I should go save him," I said without thinking and leaping from my seat.

Fallon's eyes widened. "What? Are we a superhero duo now?"

I looked at her then back across the bar where Jack's blue eyes flitted to mine. A small smirk crossed his lips, my own quirking into a grin in return.

*What the hell?*

My body pulled me like a magnet drawn to him. I practically floated around the old wooden bar until I was standing right beside his table, staring between him and the photo on the wall behind him.

The redhead was chattering nonstop in a giggly voice about something, but my focus stayed on Jack.

The guy was making my knees weak and I held on to the empty chair next to me, trying not to think about what that meant.

And now that I was in front of him, I had no idea what to do or say.

The redhead looked up, furrowing her eyebrows with a scowl. "Um, can we help you?"

I swallowed hard, licking my lips before turning to fully face Jack, and putting a hand on my hip. The first thing that came to my mind was ridiculous, but it was a game I'd played more than once with Sean when he had a lousy date in school. I figured the oldest brother could use the same escape plan.

"Jackie Poo, you didn't tell me you were leaving the office right after work. Like, I looked everywhere for you and then poof, you're gone."

Jack's smile turned into a grin as if he knew exactly how this game went. "Sorry, Grace, I thought…"

I put my hand up with a dramatic sigh and looked at the redhead. "He does this all the time, yanno? But I've gotten used to it as long as when he's done with his whiskey, he comes back and we shag like rabbits."

The redhead's face turned a darker shade than her hair, her eyes shooting daggers at Jack.

I covered my mouth and gasped. "Oh no. Was I not supposed to say that? Were you trying to shag him, too? Let me tell ya, he's not the best, but he's really easy. Just make sure he wraps it because when he has a flare up, whew!"

Jack stood up, a deep scowl on his face as he put his hand on my back, turning me in the other direction. "Sorry, Cara, it appears my assistant needs me. I think she must have been struck with fever. Have the waitress put your drinks on my tab and I'll text you later."

Cara stood up, glaring as she pushed her cleavage up. "No need. I'm leaving. You have fun with your assistant or whoever she is."

With those words, Cara stomped out of the bar.

As soon as the door shut behind her, I let out a laugh I'd been holding in for far too long.

"Shagging and flare ups? That in one of those novels you edit, or did you come up with that just to embarrass me?" Jack tilted his head slightly, his eyebrows furrowed.

"A little bit of both. It always worked well with Sean back in school. Usually, it took longer to get those girls to leave. Am I that intimidating?" I asked, putting my hand to my chest.

"Well, you succeeded in making sure I won't be getting

a second date."

I laughed, shaking my head. "Did you really even want the first one with her? You looked bored out of your mind."

A hint of a smile played on his lips. "Probably not."

He raked his fingers through his hair. "Sean used to tell me you were like his wingman, which I never believed. I always figured you two were shagging and he didn't want to tell us."

I wrinkled my nose. "Me and Sean? Ewwwwww. No thank you. I've seen the women he's dated and talk about flare ups."

Jack shook his head. "Well, I guess my date is over. Time to move on to the next one."

"I guess that's the closest I'll get to you saying I was right and thank you."

"What are you doing at the pub anyway? Didn't take you for a beer and chips girl. Or think that you'd leave Jane Pawsten that long." He nodded at a passing waitress, the smell of fried foods wafting from her tray and making my stomach rumble.

"Oh, I'm here with Fallon. Just a quick bite after work since Connor had a meeting. And Jane's at my mum's with strict instructions for her not to get near any plants," I replied.

"Is she doing better? No other run-ins with the vet?" He quirked an eyebrow.

My chest warmed, hearing the genuine concern in his tone that no one else had, not even my mum. "Yes. She's been taking her medications and all of the house plants have been put out of her reach, as well as a small wall in the garden that she barks at, wondering why it's blocking her."

He laughed. "I'd love to see her trying to hop over that. I bet she's stubborn like her owner."

I bit back a smile, trying to glare and appear mad. "I'll have you know that some people say stubbornness builds character."

He smirked in return, shaking his head as he walked with me toward the other end of the bar where Fallon was now standing next to her stool. She had her purse slung over her shoulder and her light sweater back on her shoulders.

"Looks like you saved the damsel in despair," Fallon said with a laugh then tilted her head. "What is it called if it's a man, though? Just dam? Damselo?"

"Good to see you, too, Fal," Jack said.

"As nice as it is that we're all having a good time and not at work, I have to leave. Connor is almost done with his meeting, so we're going to head home," she said quickly.

"What about your meal? Are you taking it to go? Should we order something for Connor?" Blast, now Fallon had me rambling like her.

She shook her head. "I'm sure Connor will cook something, but since the order is already in, why don't you and Jack enjoy it? He owes you another glass of wine anyway."

A flush of heat crept up my neck as Fallon winked, turning so her blond ponytail swished over her shoulder.

Was she trying to insinuate something with Jack and me? I mean that was a given, but sitting and having a drink with him could lead to other things. Things that would make him think I wanted more.

"That's not necessary. I can just get it to go," I stammered, trying to sound authoritative but my mouth had gone dry, and I could barely get the words out.

I said I didn't want to be a wife, but that didn't mean I still wasn't attracted to the guy.

"Nonsense. Sit and have a meal with me. I owe you that and something better than watered down wine," he said, pulling out my stool.

I looked between him and Fallon then finally sighed and took my seat. I guess eating the meal I ordered couldn't hurt.

And maybe he didn't have any feelings for me. Maybe he just wanted a meal with an old friend.

"Fine. But only because it's already been ordered. Then I have to get home," I said, trying to put my shoulders back and keep my composure before tucking a stray strand of my wavy brown hair behind my ear.

"I'll see you two tomorrow," Fallon called before she headed out of the pub.

Jack took the stool next to mine and signaled something to the bartender.

I frowned. "What was that about? A secret code?"

He let out a quick breath of air through his nose. "If I'm going to sit with you in my pub, I'm not going to watch you drink some shite wine."

His accent was thicker when he swore, and with the warm roll of his words a thrill of anticipation shot through me and down to my long neglected nether region.

Not now. And not with him.

The bartender sat down a flight of stemless glasses filled with different amber liquids.

"What is this?" I asked.

He picked up one glass, handing it to me, and then took one for himself. "Whiskey tasting. It was a long day at the office and an even worse attempt at a first date. I figure my knight in shining armor, or whatever you want to call yourself, deserves to find her favorite whiskey."

I swallowed hard. I couldn't remember the last time I drank whiskey and especially not with my boss. My boss, who I was starting to dislike a little less and that old childhood crush was starting to reappear.

"I don't think us getting drunk together is the best option here," I muttered, lowering my glass.

He put his hand on mine and warmth spread throughout my body, making me cross my legs and try to ignore the ache that pressed in my core. "I didn't say anything about getting drunk, *mo gra*. I'm just saying, let's enjoy one drink. I still owe you for being a gobshite at the gala."

"I think you've done more than enough. The job. Apartment. Jane…" I hesitantly looked from the glass up to his dimples and blue eyes. Blast, the man had a way of making a girl melt for him.

"Let me do this. As one friend to another. Not as your boss. Or your friend's brother. Let's try for one night to play nice at least."

Sucking in a deep breath, I looked down at the glass instead of at him.

"One drink and dinner since it's paid for," I muttered into the whiskey before downing the burning liquid.

He laughed. "It's going to be a long night if you keep drinking it like that."

I coughed, hitting my fist on my chest. "Or a very short one. That stuff is strong."

"You can't just down a fine glass of whiskey like a shot at some fraternity mixer," he said with a smirk, swirling his glass.

"Should have figured you were in a men's organization at uni," I said, picking up another glass and swirling it as he did.

"Don't tell me you're going to judge me for that, too?" he asked, putting his face closer to the glass.

I shook my head, pressing my lips together. "No. Just stating a fact."

He nodded, taking a sip. I thought I saw a hint of a frown cross his face, but it disappeared in the amber liquid.

I smirked, reaching for my almost empty wineglass by a plate of fish and chips. When did I drink so much wine? No wonder my head was getting fuzzy. I probably needed to eat. "So, were you in a men's organization? Or am I assuming?"

I popped a chip in my mouth. I couldn't remember the

last time I had the fried potatoes. Mum always made little quips about how we "both needed to watch our figure" and guilt would riddle me. Now that I was away from her, I could finally relax. I didn't have to worry about her judgey comments that made it even harder to see her on holidays when I was younger. She would wrinkle her nose at my curvy hips or new choice of fashion, like my punk phase, or that week I decided I was goth.

Not that Dad was any better. Always distracted. It wasn't until the divorce I realized it wasn't work distracting him. And Mum's quips weren't just for me. She thought if she could have that perfect figure, maybe he wouldn't have had the wandering eye.

But figuring that out came years too late.

After so many years, I was happy with the way I looked. How my life was going with a great job at a publisher and my own flat in London. Then it all came crashing down with the divorce, losing my job, and now the move to Dublin.

Now Mum and I were back on square one. I was back to the awkward little girl from the UK, hiding in her best friend's shadow.

The awkward little girl who was sharing chips and drinks with a very gorgeous man who just happened to be said best friend's brother.

"You know what they say about assuming?" He said, leaning forward, resting his hands on the arms of his chair.

I rolled my eyes, knowing that his answer meant he definitely was one of those fraternity types. "Fine. Then if we aren't going to talk about your days at uni, then let's talk about the business. Why don't you teach me how to drink whiskey?"

The words were out of my mouth before I could take them back.

He let out a single laugh and picked up a new glass.

"Very well, *mo gra*. I guess we can make this a work dinner."

"You don't need to use your flirty words with me," I said with a huff, but there was something about the way he said it to me that felt different than before. Like he wasn't just using it as a natural term of endearment, but there was a new fire behind it.

He must have felt it, too, because he cleared his throat, his eyes darting away from mine as he focused on the glass instead.

"Unlike wine, you shouldn't jam your nose into a whiskey snifter. It is a higher alcohol content than wine, and you might get tipsy just from the fumes. Instead, swirl your drink around a little and carefully whiff the scent at the top of your glass," he said, twirling his glass with extra oomph and tipping his head back slightly.

"What am I supposed to smell? Hints of chocolate? Bitterness? Bad life choices?" I asked, picking up a glass and swirling and sniffing. I didn't get much other than an alcohol smell that burned my nostrils. At least it gave me something else to focus on besides the sexy man next to me with his incredible lips emphasized by that damn dimple.

Bloody hell, I was drunker than I thought if I couldn't stop staring at his mouth.

He shook his head. "Whiskey isn't about figuring out a certain smell or color. It's about the feeling of that smell. Like snow on Christmas. It gets you nostalgic for something more."

I took in a deep breath and inhaled the scent before downing the drink.

Whiskey may bring back memories for some, but I also knew enough of it could make me forget for a while.

"Another?" he asked, holding out a full glass.

I sighed, the warmth of the liquor traveling through me.

His dark blue stare made me lose track all of the reasons I was resisting my cocky boss and every other shitty thing in my life. "Why not?"

After a few more glasses of whiskey, I was relaxed. Really laid-back for what felt like the first time in forever.

"You know, I should be thanking you for tonight," Jack said, setting his empty glass on the bar.

"I did save you from that awful date. Though, if not much has changed since I last saw you, you probably would have taken her up on a shag." I laughed, picking at my fish and chips that had now gone cold. I couldn't count the number of drinks I'd had and should have probably censored myself in front of my new boss. Even if he was my best friend's brother.

My best friend who had sent me a few texts asking what I was doing for dinner and I told him I was sharing a meal with Fallon.

Not a complete lie. I was supposed to be having dinner with her.

Now I just happened to be sitting next to his brother instead.

Jack frowned, looking at his whiskey glass instead of me. "Most girls just want a shag or what money can buy."

"Not all women want that. Of course, if they have Jack Murphy in front of them, they're probably thinking something along those lines," I said, trailing my arm in the air. As if my long arms could encompass everything from his shined loafers to his perfectly styled hair.

All of that should have stayed in my head instead. The man was every bit as gorgeous as the men I saw on romance covers and looked like he'd spent some time in the gym with the pull of his muscles against his dress shirt. I, on the other hand, hadn't seen the inside of a gym or yoga studio since we has moved to Dublin. The extra weight I had put on went mostly to my arse and hips which I was becoming more acutely aware of the longer I sat next to this man.

His lips quirked, bringing out those blasted dimples. "Most women just want to go on a date with me because they know I'm set to inherit my father's company. What they don't know is that the only way I can actually take my rightful place as head of the company is that I have to be married."

This time I did almost choke and probably spit whatever saliva was in my mouth as I leaned forward, trying to feign ignorance. "What? You're kidding? Right?"

He shook his head, taking another glass of whiskey the bartender had set out for him. "I wish I was. After Da died in April, we had a reading of the will, and there was an inheritance clause. We all have to be married within a year and stay married, or the company goes to the highest bidder on the board. Could be your granddad, which would be great for you."

"Damn. Guess I'd better see if Sean's gonna propose to me," I said, trying to lighten the conversation and not think on how my mum said the same thing. The brief thought alone twisted my gut.

"Finding a woman to shag is easy, finding someone to marry is something completely different," he said, his eyes locked on mine.

I shook my head and opened my mouth to question him, but then closed it again. Was that what he wanted from me? For the shagging or the other part?

My mind was already whirling from the alcohol, but this conversation was making my head spin.

This was the point where I needed to tell him I knew about the clause already. I didn't know if he was just talking or if he was trying to insinuate something with us. But whatever it was, it wasn't going to happen. He needed a wife and that wasn't me.

But instead of voicing anything, I just stared at the

beautiful man in front of me, who pulled a large note from his wallet and set it on the counter. "Want to get out of here?"

"What?" I asked, not sure I heard him right. Did he really think I was going to shag him?

"There's no way I'm letting you walk home alone like this," he said, standing up and putting his hand out to me.

I may have been pretty knackered, but I could still hold my ground. "Do you seriously think I'm just going to take you back to my flat and shag you after a few glasses of wine and whiskey?"

He leaned in low so his mouth vibrated on my ear. I had to bite my bottom lip to keep the moan from escaping my mouth just from the warmth of him.

"If shagging was what you wanted, I would oblige. But I'm a gentleman, Miss Evans. I'll only make you come if you ask nicely and if I know you're not completely shitefaced."

I closed my legs tightly together, feeling the soft ache just from his words. This man could turn me into a puddle of goo and prick goose bumps all over my body just from speaking. But I wasn't going to give him the satisfaction of knowing that.

He smirked. "So?"

"Let me ask Mum if Janey can stay there. I don't think I can go get her like this. And pretty sure you don't want to have a conversation with my mum," I said quickly, pulling out my phone and sending a text. He replied with something, but my brain was fuzzy and I was already texting Mum.

Me: *Mum, it looks like I'm going to have to work later than I thought. Is it all right if I pick Janey up tomorrow? Or you can have one of the maids drop her by the flat, feed her, and I'll be there later.*

I didn't mean to lie, or type that long a message. But the screen was fuzzy and I couldn't admit I just got knackered with my boss.

> Mum: *No problem at all. We'll drop her off in the morning. Say hi to Jack for me.*

I dropped my phone into my pocket book, sucked in a deep breath, and let it out as I took his waiting hand. I was pretty smashed and wasn't sure I could make it home myself in the dark. Nor could I probably take care of my dog in this state, or hungover in the morning.

What could it hurt to have someone help me out?

# Chapter Eight

JACK

"Dublin's really pretty. I always thought it felt like I was taking a step back in time with these cobblestone streets. I remember coming here to visit my grandfather as a little girl and pretending I was in Shakespeare. Though London is more Shakespeare, isn't it?" Grace asked, stopping and digging her heels into the street.

"Are you that shitefaced?" I asked, turning toward her. I didn't expect her to look up at that exact moment, those brown eyes shining in the dim light of the street lamp. How had I never noticed the golden brown of them before she walked into my office?

She used to wear so much black eyeliner you couldn't see her eyes.

Feck, she wasn't that same girl anymore.

I pushed a stray strand of hair behind her ear. Then I trailed the pad of my thumb down her jawline. I told myself I was going to keep things professional between us, no matter how much she maddened me. But when her smart mouth saved me from another bad date, I saw what a real gas she actually was. The more we drank, the more we talked, and I wondered how the hell I didn't notice her sooner. Probably because I've always been an arsehole.

Maybe if I had, I wouldn't be worrying so much about this inheritance clause. I mentally shook that out of my head. The woman barely tolerated me, and there was no way in hell I could even think like that about Sean's friend and a board member's daughter.

"Just because you got me drunk, doesn't mean I'm going to sleep with you tonight," she blurted.

I grinned. While that should have poured some cold water on the situation, it just made me want to push her even further. "First off, I think you and Fallon had a bit before I got there. Second, I would never take advantage of a drunk girl."

She scoffed. "I only had one drink, thank you very much."

I shook my head. "Well, must have been pretty strong then."

She nodded, standing a little straighter. "It was just one. It was you and that whiskey. But I'm glad you're walking me home after that and at least pretending to be a gentleman."

I laughed. "One of us has to have manners. Wouldn't want to get champagne all over our work clothes, now would we? Or maybe get into a fight with some girl at SFX because she called you a poser?"

"Oh stop," she huffed, swatting my arm gently, but her fingers stayed on my bicep, curling around the hard muscle.

"If I remember correctly, Sean had to pull you off the girl and there was a lot of hair pulling. But you told your parents it was all Sean and he took the blame."

She laughed, her grip tightening on my arm, which all the more made my whole body come alive. "Something like that."

We stayed in a comfortable silence on the short walk to her flat.

I didn't ask for permission but followed her up to the second floor. Opening the door, I turned on the light overhead. She followed, and I closed the door behind us.

I looked around the small living room that hadn't changed much since Fallon moved out. Well, aside from the small metal crate near the curtained off bedroom area.

"Grace plopped down on the couch and kicked off her heels. "It feels weirdly empty without Janey here. Maybe I should call my mum to bring her back."

"Drunk texting your mam isn't a grand idea," I said, plucking her phone from her hands and setting it on the table next to her.

Grace giggled, the first time I'd ever heard the pleasant sound come out of her. "You're probably right. She would give me a lecture about drinking and fraternizing and whatever other big words I'd say if I weren't too knackered to think of them."

I nodded, trying not to laugh at how cute she was, grinning and half-laying, half-sitting on the couch. "Just head to bed and then see Jane in the morning."

I should have turned and let her to go and left it at that. That was probably what a reasonable boss and somewhat friend would do. But instead, my curiosity and loss of my own inhibitions, had me looking around the room. My gaze stopped when I saw the silver doorway pull up bar still attached over the bathroom door.

I shook my head, thinking I would have to have a talk with Sean about leaving his stuff in the flat when he only stayed here for a few days.

Walking toward the doorway, I pulled the long pole from its attachment, wiggling the other bars to make sure they were fastened in place and not going to fall down as soon as someone walked through the door.

"You been working out?" I asked, turning to see Grace standing wide-eyed in front of me. How did she move so fast when she was just sinking into the couch?

She shook her head, her loose curls flowing against her shoulders. "I didn't even know what that was. I figured it was something structural."

Grinning, I took slow steps until we were toe to toe, the heat of her body wafting off of her and onto me. She sucked in a breath, her chest rising and falling against the top of her dress. "It's a pull-up bar with a salmon ladder attachment."

Dammit, why was I playing this game? Maybe it's because she was easier to talk to when she was shitefaced and not trying to be anyone other than herself.

"A what?" she asked.

I didn't think we'd end up back at her place. I never planned for any of this. But with her wide eyes and parted red lips, I thought I'd do at least a little explaining. And it would keep my hands busy instead of thinking about running them through her hair and wherever else I was desperate to let them roam.

Taking a few steps back to the doorway, I pulled off my dress shirt, leaving me in just a white undershirt. Her eyes roamed over the dips and curves of the shirt molding against my chest.

Feck. Why did she have to look at me like that?

I stood between the two bars then lifted my arms to position the pole in place. With a quick thrust of my hips, I jumped up, gripping the metal pole tightly as I went to the next rung.

"So you know a chin up?" I asked, dangling my legs in the air and rocking back and forth.

Her stare went from the curved V of my hips up to my

eyes, blinking slowly. "Um. I haven't done one of those since gym class in school, and even then, I don't think I actually did one."

I smirked and pulled up on the bar, my muscles constricting as I pushed the bar upward, letting out a grunt. "It's a chin up with a little extra oomph."

Her mouth hung open as I effortlessly jumped back to the floor and grinned in her direction.

"Yeah, I don't think I can do that," she muttered.

I motioned with one finger, keeping my face neutral so she wouldn't know how badly I wanted to touch her. I was trying to be a gentleman, and if working out would get her sobered up and not have a massive headache in the morning, then I'd do it.

That's what I told myself and ignored the panging deep in my chest with each little look she gave me.

"Come here."

"You're not going to try and hang me from there and do some weird BDSM thing, are you?" she asked, raising an eyebrow.

I laughed, shaking my head and motioning again. "No. Just come here and let me show you how this works."

She swallowed hard, then took a few steps forward. I put one hand on her hip, letting my fingers linger on the silky material of her dress. Feck, she smelled amazing. The sweet scent of vanilla, coffee, and the lingering whiskey on her breath was intoxicating.

I was going to be a gentleman. Being around her, just talking like we did at the pub, did something for my soul.

I just didn't want that to end yet.

I turned her around so she was facing the bar. Then I stepped to the other side so I faced her.

"I'm going to lift you so you can hang and pull up," I whispered, my lips to her ear, letting my mouth vibrate on the soft skin. She shivered slightly, a small gasp escaping her lips when I put both hands on her hips then lifted her with ease. She gripped onto the bar, breathing in shallow huffs.

"Now pull up, using your arms." I kept my hands on her waist. Her dress slightly rose, giving me a view and feel of the creamy white skin of her thighs. All I could think about was how they'd feel wrapped around me. How I shouldn't be here when she was in this state. So I kept my eyes on hers, not pushing.

"I don't know if I can do this," she whispered.

"A work out will help sober you up. You don't want to feel like shite in the morning."

"I'm not that knackered." She pouted.

"Really? Because you were just about to call your mum to bring your dog, and then you giggled."

"I said...I'm...not...that...shite...faced."

She slowly dropped down and I had to grab her legs for support so she didn't fall on her arse. Her hands went to my shoulders as I gazed into those deep golden brown eyes that had caught my attention from the moment I first saw her at the gala.

"Grace..." I warned.

"I'm not that knackered, not on the whiskey anyway, but possibly something else that has me feeling stupid enough to do this..."

She crushed her lips to mine and I held on to her, trying to fight the urge to take her right there. But I wasn't going to go where my heated body was begging me to.

Then her tongue traced the bottom of my lip. A low growl emitted from deep in my throat and I opened my mouth to her.

She tasted better than I could have imagined with the whiskey and her sweet lip gloss. Her body pressed against mine, and I tried to think how I shouldn't be there. How I should have gone home and been a gentleman. My heart and mind tugging me in two different directions.

I walked backward, carrying her across the room until I slowly leaned back onto the couch.

She straddled my lap. Her heated core pressed against my aching dick. If I wasn't lost in lust before, now I was swimming in it.

But I couldn't do this. I couldn't shag a drunk girl, or my brother's best friend and my employee for that matter. She broke our kiss, leaning back with a broad smile across her lips as she pulled off her dress, tossing it to the ground.

My gaze wandered briefly over her breasts spilling out of the lacy bra and the dips and curves that outlined her beautiful body. But then I clenched my fists at my side.

No. No. This was wrong. This was so very wrong.

"Grace…" I murmured, keeping my eyes on her face instead of where they wanted to roam.

I thought she would come back with a smart comment, but instead she squeezed her eyes shut, her body going rigid.

"Are you okay?" I asked. Maybe she really was sobering up and realizing this was a bad idea.

It was probably time I made my exit anyway, even though every part of my body was now on fire, adrenaline and anticipation coursing through me.

"I think I might throw up," she said, covering her mouth and quickly running away.

I sprang from the couch and moved aside the pieces of workout equipment before she ran past me into the small room. She crouched down.

My feet took over, and I closed the space between us. Leaning over, I pulled her wavy brown hair from her face as she dry heaved.

When she had finally finished, she moaned and muttered, "This is embarrassing. I feel like I need to puke, but I can't.

Blast. I need to sleep and sober up."

"It happens to all of us," I said in my best soothing tone.

I grabbed a washcloth from the rack and wet it in the sink, handing it to her. "Where are your pajamas?"

She stood up slowly, keeping her back to me as if I didn't just see her dry heaving into the toilet. "Um. What?"

"I don't want to go through all of your drawers but figure you want to put something on that isn't work clothes."

Her shoulders stiffened, and I tried not to admire how beautifully her back curved with a small tattoo right above the silk of her panties. One that I recognized she and Sean had gotten on a trip to China with their class when they were fourteen. Da was royally pissed when he found out they snuck off and did that.

"I'm not trying to get you naked. I just want to help you out, okay? Unlike that artist who told you your ink meant 'beautiful' and then you looked it up and found out it meant crazy."

She groaned, looking over her shoulder. "Top drawer in the dresser near my bed. And I happen to think it's a nice sentiment. The guy thought Sean and I were both crazy for each other. How wrong he was…"

I nodded, trying not to think of all of these moments she'd had with Sean and everything with me was just one feck up after the other.

I shook my head, trying not to think too hard on these thoughts. Quickly, I went back to the main room and grabbed the first pair of shorts and a top I could find, bringing it back into the bathroom.

Slowly she turned toward me, her bottom lip trembling.

Damn the woman was gorgeous. Seeing the rise and fall of her breasts as she breathed deeply, her wide eyes locked on mine, had my heart thumping rapidly, my words caught in my throat.

"Here. Do you need anything else? I can make you some toast? Or tea?"

She nodded slowly but didn't look up. "That would be nice. But you don't have to. I should just get to bed."

I didn't respond and instead made my way out of the bathroom. In the kitchen, I heated the tea kettle on the stove and found a loaf of brown bread in the fridge that was one of the only things in there. Toasting the bread with some butter, I kept my hands and my mind busy.

What was I doing?

I needed to focus on the company and finding a wife. Not whatever this was.

Yet, I couldn't move.

"Do you want to eat this in the kitchen or by the window?" I called.

I'd heard the bathroom door open but was busy filling two cups with boiling water.

Taking a few steps into the main room, I stopped when I saw her curled up in a ball on the bed, her eyes closed and sleeping soundly.

I should have left. Feck, she would probably be angry as hell if she found me there when she woke up.

But I also thought about how she would feel in the morning. And I didn't want her to get sick all over herself in the middle of the night. Before I could stop myself, I walked to the couch.

After finding a blanket, I kicked off my shoes and laid down.

I closed my eyes, pulling the blanket to my chest.

"Goodnight, Grace," I whispered.

# Chapter Nine

When I woke up, from my drunken, probably snoring slumber, I sucked in a deep breath.

My head and chest ached and not just from the whiskey.

The alcohol didn't make me forget any of the night before. All I could think about was the way Jack's muscles tightened as he worked that salmon ladder. How my body clenched, watching him. How I kept telling myself that I could totally have a one-night stand with a guy who needed a wife. Something I would never be for him.

But I couldn't think like that. I had to move on and forget it.

Looking over at the alarm clock, my eyes adjusted to the darkness. Six a.m. Still time to maybe eat the bread Jack hopefully had left out.

When I slowly sat up, my body aching with each movement, I noticed a glass of water and bottle of aspirin on the nightstand. I quickly took two pills, downing them with the water before I stood up, my joints popping.

I wondered how many other girls Jack had done these hangover cures for. And if he'd bring it up today at work. Lord knows he never forgot about the almost arrest and that was eight years ago.

But all my thoughts stopped when I got to the bathroom and saw my face in the mirror. I didn't have time to think about anything other than washing my face, brushing my teeth, showering, and trying to not look like a raccoon on crack with my makeup smeared face and frizzy hair.

I'd tried to shag Jack looking like this? Was that before or after I almost puked?

Bollocks, I was never drinking whiskey again.

When I finally opened the bathroom door with my hair and makeup done, dressed, and feeling slightly human, I heard the faint sound of voices.

The hair on the back of my neck stood on end. This wasn't technically my flat, but I thought I'd have some privacy. Slowly, I peered around the corner

"Thanks, Mrs. O'Hanlon, Have a good day."

I recognized that voice, and when the front door shut, I quickly pulled back, pressing my body against the bathroom wall.

Blast. What was he doing here? Was my embarrassing night not enough? Now was he going to gloat?

"Sleep well, Grace?" His voice carried through the small room.

"Spying on me? I thought this was my flat and you couldn't just walk in," I said, finally walking out of the bathroom.

Jack was still in his dress shirt and trousers from the night before, smiling, and holding a white paper bag. "Thought you might want some breakfast."

He brought me food? What?

What kind of guy does that after he watches you get sick?

And apparently stays the night…somewhere…close…

A guy who is a decent human being and not the devil incarnate, I guess.

"Have a seat." He walked toward the small table by the window and pulled out a stool, effectively knocking me out of my thoughts.

"You didn't need to get me breakfast…" I said, looking at the Styrofoam container of food. My stomach was growling. Blast, why couldn't I control any of my reactions today?

"I did, and I should be a proper gentleman and make you a cuppa," he said, heading toward the kitchen.

"A proper gentleman who showed up at my apartment in his clothes from the night before," I blurted, unable to stop myself. I wondered if he really did leave another girl that morning. If I was now the epitome of repulsion.

Why did I even try anything with him? I'll blame the whiskey and salmon ladder.

He laughed slightly and sat the kettle on the stove. "I stayed here last night. Thought that was obvious."

Blood rushed to my head. He stayed here? He saw me at my worst then still stayed? I didn't know whether to vomit or swoon. "I puked and passed out. A proper gentleman would have left me to my misery."

He stilled, then slowly turned away from the stove. His dark blue eyes bore into me as he crossed the room to stand in front of me.

A gasp escaped my lips, partially from shock and partly from the nearness of him. It had been so long since I'd been with anyone, but he especially did something that had every part of my body come alive with one little touch.

"I did nothing improper. You were bolloxed, and I wanted to make sure nothing else happened to you, so I slept on the sofa. You can be pissed at me all you want, but I'm not apologizing for doing what I thought was right."

I glared, trying to keep my resolve. No man had ever done anything for me like that. Hell, no person had.

Just because we shared a drunken, yet very explosive kiss that still made me warm from thinking about it, didn't mean anything. I wasn't going to get involved with my boss.

"I should head out. I have a meeting this morning, so I'll be in later. Have my assistant hold my calls, will ya?" He winked like this was just an ordinary occurrence. Like we were old pals.

"Thanks for breakfast," I muttered, looking at my food instead of the dimple on his cheek. The one I had kissed just the night before. The one I would never, ever kiss again.

I didn't breathe again until the door shut and I knew he was gone.

"What the hell had I gotten myself into?" I whispered to no one in particular, since I was by myself, again.

I gasped when my answer came with the front door opening and Jane Pawsten sprinting in, followed by my mother and Grandmum.

Shit. Just what I needed.

"Gracie, was that Jack Murphy I just saw in the hall?" Mum's voice carried through the room until she was standing in front of me, hands on her hips.

Grandmum stood beside her in a zebra print shirt dress with sparkly sequin leggings. Mum said her crazy outfits could be the start of dementia or something more serious. Her grand excuse that we needed to be closer and move to Dublin, that I went along with, knowing she wanted to save face for everyone else. But I think Grandmum just always went to the beat of her own drum. I wish everyone could always be as free as she was.

"Bloody hell, Mum, his company owns the building. And what are you doing here? I thought I'd come get her after work." I stood up and went to the kitchen, grabbing Jane's food bowl and water so I'd have something to do with my hands and not face the two women.

"Well, we were just taking a walk and thought we'd stop by and see how you were feeling. You know, since you were out all night with your coworker, but then I see Jack walking out. Do normal business owners check up on their assistants in their buildings or is there something you want to tell me about Jack? Maybe that you considered what I told you?"

"What are we talking about? Is Grace pregnant? Is she carrying the billionaire's baby? I saw that in a book once. Or maybe it wasn't a book, and it was a movie...one of those dirty videos from the computer..." Grandmum said.

"Mother," Mum snapped, turning sharply toward the old woman who just shrugged, fluffing her short gray hair.

I sighed, taking in the overwhelming smell of Mum's floral perfume and shutting my eyes. This was not the conversation I wanted to have. Not now. Not ever. Especially not in front of Grandmum. "Mum, I'm not going to seduce a man and drop him just to get the company."

"I'm sure your cousin Lacey would. She is a gold digger that one. Is that what they call it?" Grandmum added.

Hearing my cousin's name made the hair on the back of my neck stand on end.

Lacey was better than me at everything. She had flawless skin, beautiful curls, made honor roll, and was a talented athlete. She was Jack's age, and the two had an on-again-off-again thing in boarding school and uni.

I still wasn't sure I even liked the man. But it still left a sour taste in my mouth.

"I'm sure Lacey has better things to do than chase after a man," I quipped, pouring some kibble into Jane's bowl.

"She is coming into Dublin for business soon. She'll probably be in for tea. And if there is something going on with you and Jack, I can make sure she won't be around when he is. Though if you really are falling for him, maybe your cousin would have a few choice words about being in love with a man who wants nothing but business," Mum said.

I sighed. We always thought father was in love with his work, too. All the late nights at the office were a front for one of his many side flings. Something Mum and I found out way too late.

"I have to get ready for work. And I'm trying to keep things professional between Mr. Murphy and me."

I turned in time to see Mum's tight smirk. "Gracie, dear, I know you've always had this little crush on the oldest Murphy, but do you think spending the night with him this early is wise? Is this part of a plan to seduce him so he doesn't get married and Grandfather can get the company? If it's not…darling…I don't want you to get hurt."

She blinked slowly and I saw concern flutter across her usually stoic face.

I never came right out and said how much her and Dad's divorce ruined my thoughts of marriage, but I think she knew. And she didn't want her daughter to get hurt like she had.

"He…he…was…just…I…was…" I sputtered, trying to think of a response but my mind went completely blank.

Grandmum cackled, pointing a crooked finger at me. "Gracie has a boyfriend!"

"He's not my boyfriend, Grandmum."

Mum patted my arm. "Gracie, I know you may think you know what's best and it was kind of him to take care of little Janey…"

Mum's eyes trailed to the little dog who had buried her face in her food bowl. "But I worry about you. I know you work on romance novels and maybe you still believe in a happily ever after, even with everything we've been through." She sighed. "I don't want you to get hurt in all of this, Gracie. Maybe it was silly to even bring all of this up."

I shook my head. "It's fine, Mum. It's not like I'm actually falling for the guy. He doesn't even like me like that. He's just trying to find any woman he can."

I nodded to myself, even though her words punched me hard in the gut. Of course he didn't want to be with me. He needed someone easy to get along with and someone who would fall into the role of his wife. I was neither of those things to him. Something that was hard to even admit to myself.

Janey snorted at my feet then pawed my shoes so I picked her up. "I'm going to have to take Jane for a walk before work, then I can bring her back over on my way out."

Mum waved her hand. "Nonsense, Gracie, we aren't going to make you go out of your way. We'll stay for a cuppa then take Janey back to Grandmum's."

Grandmum eyed the little white bag on the table before opening it and pulling out a pastry. "Oh, bannock, your man knows the good stuff."

"He's not my man, Grandmum."

She smiled. "Of course he isn't."

I sighed, there was no point in trying to argue with the old woman or my leery Mum. Not when I wasn't even sure what was going on with Jack and me anyway.

But, I hated to admit it, Mum did have a point. No use getting involved or even trying. No matter if my heart was tugging me in a different direction.

If I thought things were screwed earlier this morning, now things just got twenty times more bloody complicated.

# Chapter Ten

I took the longest, coldest shower of my life, then got dressed and headed to the office.

But before I made my way through the famous wrought iron Murphy gates, I stopped at the same café I met Grace at for our meeting that was interrupted by Jane Pawsten and the vet.

She was sitting at her desk, not bothering to look up from the computer when I approached and sat a Styrofoam cup of tea in front of her.

"I promised you a cuppa that I never got to finish making," I whispered, leaning in so only she could hear and not any of the gossiping employees.

No acknowledgment from the strong-willed girl, but I accepted that. A challenge never stopped me before.

Tapping on her chair, I headed into my office where Connor was perched on the corner of my desk.

I scowled, glancing at my watch. The last person I wanted

to see was my smirking brother. "We aren't supposed to meet for another hour."

He laughed as I breezed past him, hanging my suit jacket on the leather wingback chair.

"I'm not here on business-business, but I think we both know that."

I had a feeling a certain blonde former assistant may have done some talking. But I feigned innocence and shook my head. "Not sure what you mean."

He stood up, crossing his arms over his chest. "You know exactly what I mean. I'm talking about you spending the evening with your assistant who also happens to be Sean's best mate. By the shifty look in your eyes, I'm guessing the drinks at the pub turned into something more. Especially since the barista at the café told me she saw you right before me this morning. The only reason you'd be in the neighborhood that early and not at work is if you never went home."

I swore under my breath. I knew I should have just gone home or to SuperMacs down the road. But I just had to be a gentleman. And I couldn't fight the feeling that I wanted to see Grace again that morning before work with something more than just banter.

"So is she the one?" Connor asked, his voice raising slightly with elation.

I shook my head. "The one? Are you mad? She's my assistant. We barely know each other."

He held up a finger. "Technically you've known each other since we were kids, so she'd be a perfect match. Board wouldn't even question a proposal, and by the way she looks at you, there's a thin line between wanting to fight you and wanting to feck your brains out."

I scowled at his brash choice of words. He didn't know anything about Grace's and my relationship. She wasn't just one of these birds I'd take home from the pubs for a quick shag.

Though I didn't know what she was either and that's what had my stomach twisting in knots.

"There is nothing going on between us. I walked her home from the pub because she was a bit knackered. And I don't know what the hell you're getting at talking about her as *the one*. Marriage isn't just something you can throw at a girl after a few weeks."

His body went rigid. He and Fallon had known each other through phone calls and emails for six months before they met in person. Then within three months they were engaged and married. Which also conveniently went hand in hand with the marriage clause.

"You do what you want, but this isn't just about the company or what is written on a piece of paper. This is about a girl who you should give a proper chance to."

I smirked. "Thanks for the advice, but I know what I'm doing. And I don't mix business with pleasure."

At least as far as he knew.

A broad grin spread across his face. "Then I guess you saw who our two o'clock meeting is with?"

I hadn't even opened my computer or looked at my phone all morning but had a feeling I wasn't going to like what I saw.

Without glancing back at his smug face, I headed to my desk, logged onto the computer, and opened my calendar.

I froze as soon as I saw the name on the two o'clock meeting.

Lacey Walsh with Poppy Wines.

Last time I saw Lacey was at uni when I was going to surprise my on-again, off-again girlfriend with flowers after our last finals. Only I was the one who got the surprise when she promptly said it wasn't working and broke it off.

I didn't think I was in love, but ever since then, I'd never been with another woman for more than a night.

Until Grace…if that counted.

Now I'd have to sit with her at the conference table.

"I guess by the way your eyes are bulging, you hadn't seen the meeting?"

I looked past my smirking brother to the closed office door. Without a second thought, I walked around my desk and opened the door.

Fallon and Grace sat at her desk, both lifting their heads as I approached.

"Miss Evans, can you join me at my two o'clock meeting? I'll need someone to take notes."

Her eyes narrowed for a brief moment before she turned to her computer. "I can carve out some time, I guess."

She smirked, her long fingers tapped on the keys and then froze, mid-stroke, as she stared at the screen.

I wanted to come up with a quick retort; then I saw her face turn white. I racked my brain, wondering what the hell she could have seen.

That's when recognition finally dawned on me.

These two were cousins.

Lacey used to visit her Granddad's in the summer when she wasn't off in the American Hamptons or wherever else her parents sent her to. Grace was the only one who visited every summer and holiday. She was a permanent fixture. Always running around in the back with Sean while Lacey wouldn't even look at the sun unless it was artificial from a tanning booth.

I didn't even notice through my reminiscing haze that Connor had followed me out of the room. That is, until he perched himself on the desk next to Fallon. "Excited to see your cousin? Been a while since I've seen her, but I'm guessing she's still the same crazy bird she was in school. No offense, Jack, just never know what you saw in her."

"Yeah. Well, we all do stupid things when we're younger

and sometimes even when we're older," I muttered, glancing at Grace who wouldn't even look in my direction.

Connor laughed. "Did you forget she was Grace's cousin? Maybe it's time to cut back on the whiskey."

I blinked, my throat going dry as I cleared it. I wasn't usually a man at a loss for words, but this was a situation that warranted saying everything and nothing.

"It's fine, Connor. I can deal with Lacey, and if Jack needs a bodyguard, I've got that, too." Grace smiled sweetly, the first time I'd seen that quirk of her lips since before she kissed me last night.

What the hell was going through this girl's head?

"Thank you, Grace. I'll see you at two," I said huskily with a nod, licking my lips to regain some moisture.

With that I went back to my office, closed the door, and tried to figure out what the hell I was going to do at two o'clock.

• • •

Lacey Walsh hadn't aged a day. The tall blonde stood at one end of the conference table in a black, sleeveless dress with her hair falling in a pin-straight line to her shoulders.

While Grace was curvy, Lacey was the opposite. She was thin as a lollipop, but there was nothing sweet at all about her frozen smile and skeptical green eyes.

"Jack, Connor, thanks for meeting with me." Lacey's black heels clicked on the wooden floor as she took long strides toward us.

She may have been speaking to my brother and me, but her glare zeroed in on Grace.

As soon as Lacey shook our hands, she leaned over and stiffly hugged my wide-eyed assistant.

"Grace. Granddad told me you were working here,

though I assumed you'd be in an editorial role. Are you Jack's assistant?" Her very thin eyebrows raised high on her head as she pulled back and looked between us.

Grace opened her mouth, but I interjected.

"She's actually training to be our new head of purchasing. That's why I asked her here today," I blurted.

Maybe this was why Grace had looked at her cousin's name like it smelled foul.

Ever since we were younger, Lacey always carried herself like she was better than everyone. An urge to protect Grace took over, but by the way she held her shoulders back and smirked those red lips, I knew she could hold her own. Though that didn't stop me from helping the girl out.

"Really?" Lacey tilted her head.

I willed myself not to scowl, putting my arm around Grace's shoulder and squeezing it like we were old pals, even though she winced under my touch. Something that gutted me more than I cared to admit.

"We saw each other again at a gala, and after hearing about her experience as an editor in London, I knew I had to have her on the team."

Connor laughed. "Yeah, you can say that first meeting was a smashing success. But now we're here, so let's get started."

I was thankful for Connor's interruption and smart mouth, for once.

I took a seat in between Grace and Connor at one side of the table while Lacey stood on the other.

In front of her was a display of brightly colored wine bottles and a few neon yellow notebooks that she handed to each of us with a matching pen. I looked down at the fluorescent books in our hands, my gaze trailing to Grace's red nail polish. Her hands shook slightly as she sat down the notebook and picked up her tablet. She opened up a document with different color-coded spreadsheets.

What did this girl have up her sleeve?

"As you know, I'm the marketing and sales director for Poppy Wines."

She uncorked a white bottle and poured a small amount into three different glasses with a brightly colored logo etched on the side. "I know Murphy's Pubs focuses on your beer and whiskey. But a wine straight from the UK can attract more clients especially to your U.S. locations. Wine drinking is up in the states and everyone is looking for the best new taste."

She placed the glasses in front of us and put her hands together, beaming like she'd just won a beauty pageant.

I put the glass to my lips, but before I could take a drink, Grace's voice stopped me.

"Lacey, correct me if I'm wrong, but while the UK is a huge wine consumer only about one percent of all wines are produced there. Due in part to a colder climate and that grapes will only produce a good crop two in every ten years."

I put my drink down, trying to hide my smile toward my quick-witted assistant. She was ballsy that was for sure. I guess she did more research than I, or my former assistants did before this meeting and that explained all of her spreadsheets. She was more prepared than even I was and I had to give her credit for that. A new sense of pride swelled within me.

Lacey opened and closed her mouth like a fish before she nodded. "That is correct, Grace. But our winery in Surrey is over four-hundred acres and has been able to keep up production. Especially with the rise in more pleasant weather."

Lacey opened a dark purple bottle, pouring a small amount into another glass with the same logo etched on the side, but this time her hands and words slightly shook. "We're also proud producers of Wrotham Pinot which have survived British winters for over two-thousand years."

Grace's lips formed a thin line, not even looking at the new glass in front of her. "I'm guessing, for the grapes to survive, then these have to be greenhouse grown? Hybrids if you will?"

"Well, yes, but you see—" Lacey started, but Grace interjected.

"How can you charge wines at market rate when you're clearly using cheap coal and glass houses to produce your wines? And what is this on the label? Does it say bottle fermenting? This isn't a hobby farmer in his backyard making gin; this is supposed to be a company you want people to invest in. How can you expect a billion-dollar pub industry to serve their customers this?"

Grace shook her head. "This may just be my opinion, but most people who go to a Murphy's Pub aren't ordering a glass of wine. The less than one percent who do aren't going to cover the cost of spending twelve euro a bottle on your swill when the Americans can just go up the street and get a two-buck chuck as they call it."

I'd never seen Lacey off her game but her face visibly flushed. She let out a stuttered huff, grabbing and sifting through a leather portfolio to shoot some facts our way.

But everything she came back with, Grace had more ammunition.

Connor leaned toward me, his voice low, even though the women weren't even paying attention to us. "Maybe we really should hire her in purchasing."

"Trying to rid me of another assistant?" I asked, crossing my arms over my chest.

"Hey, if it helps the company." He shrugged.

When Lacey and Grace had seemed to put a halt to their quarrel, we all stood from the table, and I extended my hand to Lacey.

"Thank you for coming today. Grace, Connor, and I need

to crunch some numbers and present this to the board before we can get back to you with a final decision."

Lacey fluttered her long eyelashes, leaning forward slightly, so I got a full view of the plastic breasts pressing against the fabric of her dress. "It was good to see you, Jack. It's been a long time. Maybe we can catch up, and you can actually taste some of this wine before you decide. I'll be in town for a little while, if you want to grab dinner."

She pulled a slim case from her pocketbook and grabbed a white card, placing it in my hand.

"I'll make sure this goes with the rest of our business cards," Grace quipped, plucking the paper from my hand and stuffing it into the portfolio with her tablet.

Lacey smirked, nodding toward Grace. "Please do. And I'm sure I'll see you at Granddad's for tea on Sunday."

She turned on her heel, walking toward the door but glanced over her shoulder as she stood just steps away. "Oh, and Jack, you're more than welcome to join us."

With that she was out of the door, leaving the three of us in the conference room.

"I should get back to work as well. Gotta type up these notes," Grace said, waiting a few beats before Lacey was surely out of earshot.

"And while you're doing that, I'll see about openings in purchasing," I said.

Both Connor and Grace side-eyed me, and I just smiled.

Part of me wanted to keep the spitfire for myself as an assistant. But she was over-qualified. That had been more than evident in this meeting.

That said, I was in no rush to see her go.

# Chapter Eleven

GRACE

Bloody hell.

At least my semester of Bacchus study and a few manuscripts about winery owners had come in handy. But now Lacey was probably running off to tell her mum and mine that I was some purchaser and would soon be corrected to look like a fool.

During the meeting, Jack looked at me different than he had in our previous encounters. It wasn't lustful like at the gala or even scowling like I was used to. Was he actually proud?

Connor had another meeting to attend to which left me and Jack alone, walking together back to the office. Something that had the butterflies in my stomach fluttering too fast for my liking.

"I don't need to see any of your notes if everything you said was true in the meeting," he said, breaking the sharp silence we'd had since he dropped the bombshell about looking for other openings for me. What did that even mean?

By the way he and Lacey had looked at each other, I had a feeling it was more than the "fling" she liked to call it. Now was he going to drop me as his assistant and look for somewhere else to put me? Because of a set of plastic tits who didn't even know what she was talking about with her company?

Ugh.

Jealousy seethed within me and I had to get a grip. Jack wasn't mine and he never would be. I should just take what he would offer and move up in the company.

"Um, well," I stammered, trying to think of the right words but my tongue was twisted.

What the bloody hell was this man doing to me?

We reached his office and then he turned to me. "I've never seen Lacey so flustered or put in her place. But, hell, my brother is right about you, you're definitely too damn good to be just my assistant."

His voice fell slightly as he ran a hand through his hair. The hair I had run my fingers through while his tongue met mine. The hair that felt like silk between my fingers. Before I almost threw up on those fancy shoes he wore.

Oh my God, I had to get a grip.

"Now I don't know what the feck I'm going to do without you," he muttered.

My reflexes were quicker than my mind, and I grabbed his warm hand. "I'm not going anywhere."

I gasped as soon as I realized what I was doing and yanked my wrist back. "I mean, I'm not going for another position in the company right now. I've only just started. I'm not even done with training."

His lips pursed. "We both know I can do most of my own assistant duties. It's just easier having someone paying attention to the scheduling."

He had a point. But I'd miss his lips.

What the hell? I couldn't think about Jack or what else I thought about his mouth and sinfully seductive smile. But the more my mind wandered, the more I had butterflies practically doing somersaults in my stomach. And other places for that matter.

No. No. No.

Jack needed a wife and that definitely wasn't me. No matter how much it hurt to even think that.

I sucked in a breath, narrowing my eyes to right myself and think about him as the cocky bastard from when we were younger instead of the sweet man who held my hair back. "If this is some attempt to get me to move to another department, so it would be fine with HR if you hooked up with my cousin or with me, or both for that matter, then I'm here to tell you that's not going to work."

A low groan emitted from deep in his throat and he leaned in, his lips mere inches from mine, and I could almost taste the mint on his breath and feel the heat of his body. He always had me hyperaware of his presence, but now every part of me ached to be touched. Something I couldn't let him see, even though my whole body vibrated.

"You can put on this act all you want, but we both know you're here because you need a job and I need an assistant. So this worked out for both of us."

I let out a deep breath, expecting a sexier remark than the truth that hit me right in the gut. "Then why would you try to push me into another position?"

He raked his fingers through his hair, pieces sticking up all over. It made the usually polished man carry a sexier air to have it a little messy. "What do you want me to tell you? That I curse myself every day that I made the wrong impression on you at the gala? That I've been trying to make it up to you? How I was trying to be a gentleman but when you kissed me,

I almost lost all resolve."

Heat flushed my cheeks and all the way down to my core at his words. I licked my lips, trying to regain some moisture and composure. "We had both been drinking...and..."

His rough hands went to my chin, tilting it up so I met his burning blue eyes. "Use whatever excuse you want, but we both know there's something between us. I don't know if us working together will push us closer together or tear us apart. Either way, I'm not going to stop you from reaching your potential with the company or wherever you go. That's how much I care about you."

His words panged something deep in my chest that I'd never felt before. Caring? How could he care about me when he didn't even know me?

But he and the Murphy family knew me better than most people, even more than my so-called older cousin and parents. But could I really fall for him?

No.

He needed a wife to get his company. Even if we tried to work it out, I wasn't a wife. The thought panged me as soon as it crossed my mind.

I could be a fling. I could be a distraction. But both of those things would cause him to lose the company if he didn't find a real wife.

When his fingers trailed from my chin to the curve of my neck, all thoughts left me. All I could focus on was the rough pad of his thumb against my heated body. "I'm not the same arsehole I was when we were younger. Still a right gobshite, but that boy you knew back then isn't the same man I am now. I wish you would see that. I've tried so hard for you to see that."

He was right. I couldn't deny it. The cocky boy who wouldn't give me or anyone else a second glance was different now.

His fingers grazed the sensitive flesh right below my neck and my lips parted with a small sigh.

My eyes stayed on him as he slowly moved closer, pressing his lips to mine.

I gave in to his touch, and he moved with determination. One hand rested near my cheek and the other wrapped around my waist. He pulled me flush against him, deepening our kiss as I gasped into his hungry mouth.

He gripped my waist, his erection pressed against my stomach.

My mind was saying this was wrong and I needed to stop him, but my hands were saying something completely different as I buried my fingers in his hair and nibbled on his bottom lip.

Between every bite and swipe of his tongue, I became more drunk on his touch. More than I'd been on the whiskey.

My brain fogged and all I could focus on was him against me. How we just fit together, no matter that he was at least six inches taller than me and I had to stand on my tippy-toes, even in heels.

He must have noticed my straining because he gripped my arse, lifting me up to press me against the wall.

I wrapped my legs around his middle, getting him as close to me as I could. Not caring that I was in a skirt and my damp panties pressed against his straining erection.

I was too lost in the moment. Everything was right when I didn't think for once. It was just him, me, and his gorgeous lips.

If he would have taken me against the wall right there, I wouldn't have objected.

I would have forgotten all about him needing a wife and not something casual, which was all I could ever be.

But the universe spoke before any of that could happen when a knock came at the door.

We both jumped apart. My feet hit the floor, and I tugged my skirt down and straightened my blouse. Jack ran his thumb across the bite mark I left on his lip with a cocky smile before adjusting his tie. There was still a slight smattering of lip-gloss at the corner of his mouth.

Leaning forward, I pressed my thumb to his soft lips. He looked down at me, not saying a word while I tried to remove the offending red mark.

He lightly kissed my thumb and squeezed my hand, leaving a tingle that bloomed all the way from my thumb to my toes.

He opened the door to a smirking Connor who was standing with Fallon. "Should we come back another time?"

Jack shook his head, and I wondered if his brother noticed that it was definitely more than pleats in his trousers. "No need. Grace and I were just discussing a new position."

Connor laughed, shaking his head. "I don't want to know about your sex life."

My cheeks burned, wondering if he had heard any of our rumblings. Hell, what if Sean found out about Jack and me from Connor? Would he be pissed if he knew we were hooking up? Or throw us a ticker tape parade? I didn't even want to have this discussion with him about my love life. Or whatever this was.

Blast, this was getting complicated.

I frowned, keeping my head down and pushing past Connor to stand on the other side of the doorway. "We were discussing the job in purchasing, but as I already told Mr. Murphy, I'm not ready to move on yet."

I glanced at Jack over my shoulder before circling my desk. He had a small smile on his face that matched my own. "We can talk more about that later."

I kept my head down, for fear my cheeks were completely scarlet.

After Connor closed the door, I took my seat and Fallon eyed me skeptically as she sat down, as well.

"Sorry I was late. He just had some questions for me," I muttered, putting my shaking hands on my lap.

She laughed. "If I could sing, or even hum, I'd sing that song from that one movie. You know the one with the French girl who lives in a castle as this guy's slave and some pots sing to her? It's on the tip of my tongue. Why can't I think of it?"

I shook my head. "Are you talking about Beauty and the Beast?"

She snapped her fingers then pointed at me. "Yes. That's the one. Which is kind of funny because Connor always refers to Jack as beastly and you're, well not French, but from Britain. Dammit, I'm rambling again."

I shook my head. "The original French tale is nothing like the animated version from the 1990s. In the story, Belle becomes the mistress of the castle and the beast her slave. His choice."

Fallon put her hands up, her eyes wide. "Whoa, didn't say I wanted to know what you and Jack do behind closed doors."

I rolled my eyes. "There's nothing like that going on between Jack and me."

"Really? Because your face was red and flustered when you opened his door, and Jack had lipstick on the side of his mouth."

She stifled a laugh, but every hair on the back of my neck stood on end. If my face wasn't already red, it was now probably brighter than the lip gloss that was supposed to stay on my lips all day. Blasted American sellers and their claims. And blast that I didn't get all of it off his mouth.

"There's no need to be embarrassed, and it's not like I'm going to go and blab to the world that you and Jack have something going on."

I shook my head. "We don't have anything going on."

She smacked her lips. "I shouldn't pry, but something went on in that meeting with your cousin. And I'm sensing there are some ill feelings between the two of you or something, if your reaction to seeing her name in the calendar means anything."

I let out a breath, my shoulders falling. "You have *no* idea."

"You totally don't have to talk about it. We can just go back to work."

I sighed. "No, no. It's fine. It's just…well…weird. She was always the better looking one who got the better grades and had parents who bragged about her extracurriculars. I was just the geek who spent most of my time studying at boarding school. During summers when I was hanging out with Sean, she was off doing global ambassador work or whatever else her dad found."

"That doesn't even sound real. It's like something a girl writes down to pad her beauty pageant application," she muttered.

I laughed, covering my mouth for fear I'd snort. When I finally was able to let out a breath, I moved my hands to my lap.

"That pretty much describes my cousin, and why she and Jack made this perfect couple."

"Yeah, but that was college or whatever when they dated. People change."

I nodded. "I guess you're right."

"I know I'm right. Let's move forward and get you finished with training. If Connor's right, you might be moving on to the next position soon. If that's the case, I'm making you train the next poor girl who sits in this seat."

I sighed. "Not you, too."

She laughed, tossing her hair over her shoulder. "Just repeating what I heard."

• • •

It had been almost a week exactly since the meeting with Lacey where Jack brought up the new position…then put me in a new position against his office wall.

A memory that had starred in many of my dreams, only to wake up and realize we'd never do that again. Everything had stayed platonic, which I wasn't sure I was happy about or not. That is, until Jack emerged from his office, a broad grin on his face.

"What are you doing this weekend?" he asked casually, leaning against my desk.

"Um…I'd have to look at my schedule," I said, knowing I had absolutely nothing going on but tea with my mother that I'd love to avoid.

"Clear your schedule. This is work related. I'll pick you up at ten." He nodded as if I'd just agree to whatever he asked. Well, he picked the wrong girl if he thought that.

"Excuse me?" I leaned forward, unsure I heard him right.

"Excuse what? I told you this was work. I need an assistant to accompany me. Don't get your knickers in a twist. There's nothing nefarious that can happen on a Saturday morning before noon."

Heat rose to my face, and I cleared my throat, hoping he didn't see my small crack of a smile.

His fingers drummed the corner of my desk. "So I'll see you at ten then?"

I opened my calendar app on the computer. Jack had an event that was locked from ten to three on Saturday. What was he up to? My heart sped up at the thought of some alone time with him and I tried to clamp it down.

*This is your boss, Grace. That's it. You're not wife material. You're not what he needs.*

Blast, even saying that mantra in my head had my chest tightening, but I couldn't let that show as I offered a small smirk. "I guess I can fit you in."

# Chapter Twelve

I couldn't stop thinking about Grace's lips. And the rest of her body.

How she felt pressed against me.

I'd been with plenty of women in my lifetime, but none had made me feel alive like she did.

I needed a wife if I wanted to keep Murphy's Pub and I should have been out there, continuing to look for other women to date and marry.

But the moment Grace spoke up in the meeting, I knew that this woman cared about the company just as much as we did. That there was something about her that was worth keeping around, even if it wasn't as my assistant.

This little trip today was research to look further into the ideas she'd brought into the meeting. She just didn't know that yet. Or how much I was mixing business with pleasure.

After parking in my spot in the underground garage at Murphy's Pub headquarters, I made the short trek to a little café and picked up chocolate croissants and lattes. The flat was two blocks from work, which made the building the perfect real estate investment for Murphy's. The board had talked about eventually turning it into shops or something that would bring in more revenue, but as long as a Murphy was still at the helm, I wasn't going to kick anyone out of the building they lived in.

Especially not the sexy Brit who I couldn't stop thinking about.

I knew she'd be rightfully pissed if I just walked in again. Though I loved to see her narrow those caramel-colored eyes and pout, I decided instead to go for texting first.

Standing outside her door, I pulled my phone out of my pocket.

Me: *Hungry? I've got something hot and sweet waiting for you.*

Her response was fast and of course, quick-witted.

Grace: *If this is a come on, even though we're off work hours, I could still report you to HR.*

I rolled my eyes. We were past the HR comments.

Me: *Open the door and see what kind of treat you'll find.*

The door slowly creaked open, and instead of Grace happily jumping into my arms, the little furry mutt pounced at my feet. She yapped and turned in little circles like she hadn't seen me in years.

"Janey, leave the poor man alone," Grace scolded, picking up the little furball which gave me an excuse to let my eyes roam over her body. The little blue dress hugging her hips had me thinking about anything other than work.

I'd had one date since I first saw Grace at the gala and she started working at Murphy's. One that ended very badly.

I was supposed to be looking for a wife, not lusting after my assistant. If I hurt her in any way, Sean would have my arse. He may be younger than I was, but I'd seen him on the rugby field, and I was pretty sure he could break every bone in my body. Which was why I wondered why I was so determined to play this very dangerous game.

She smiled.

Bloody hell. Yes. That was why.

"I hope that coffee is for me and you're not just teasing," Grace called, walking into the flat and knocking me out of my daze.

I figured that was my cue to follow, shutting the door behind us while she grabbed a bowl of kibble for the dog.

"I'd never tease, *mo gra*," I said, setting the croissants on the counter before handing her a steaming foam cup.

"Why are you being so nice and so chipper this early on a Saturday?" she asked before taking a sip of her drink. Her lips slightly quirked into a smile after she tasted the hot liquid.

"What's not to be happy about? It's a beautiful day, and I get to spend it with my cranky assistant." I put my arms out, as if I could encompass the room and all of beautiful Dublin.

"Funny." She grabbed a sweater off the coat rack, putting it on and spoiling my wonderful view of where that low neckline ended. "Where are we going anyway? Somewhere I'm underdressed for?"

"Your outfit is perfect. Now come on, let's eat something then take Janey for a quick walk. Maybe next time we'll bring her to the meeting. But today, we'll pass and we don't want to be late."

She quirked an eyebrow. "Jane Pawsten to a business meeting? Next time? And now you two are on a nickname basis?"

I smiled down at the little furball, wagging her tail as she looked up at me. "She'd be a great negotiator. Look at that face. You can't say no to her."

Crouching down, I scratched behind her ears and she closed her eyes, her tail now thwapping at full speed.

"I can take her for a quick walk and then we can head out, let me just have another sip of my drink first," she replied, putting the drink to her lips.

I shook my head, standing at full height. "I can take her. Where is her leash?"

"You? Take Jane on a walk?"

"I may have never had a pet but I'm sure I can walk a dog."

A small smile crossed Grace's lips as pulled out a little pink leash and harness, handing that to me with one hand and holding out a little green baggy in the other.

"What's that for?"

"To pick up poo. She hasn't gone yet this morning, so it should be a good one."

She could *not* be serious.

"You want me to bend over and pick up the dog's shite?"

"I wouldn't be a responsible dog owner if I just let it sit in the street." She leaned over, hooking the leash and harness on the wiggly little pup. "How would you like it if you were walking into the office and you stepped on a big mound in your shiny loafers?"

"That would be a stink to get out of leather."

She bit down on her bottom lip as her shoulders shook, probably holding back a laugh. "I can take her. It's no problem."

"A Murphy always keeps his word, even if that word means picking up shite," I said, grabbing the bag and looking down at the dog.

"Come on, Janey."

The little dog barked and then pranced along next to me as we headed out to the front of the building.

• • •

After Jane Pawsten barked at every leaf that blew by, the Danes next door, and then finally did her business, I made my way back up the stairs and into the flat.

Grace raised an eyebrow, her eyes glued to me as Jane ran past to her water bowl and I made my way to the bathroom sink.

"You really walked my dog and picked up her business?" she asked, standing in the doorway.

I smirked, catching her gaping mouth in the reflection of the bathroom mirror. "Ah. Wouldn't want anyone to step on it, though she had to stop long enough to quit barking at these two Danes and do her business."

She nodded. "Yeah. Those dogs are a pain in the arse. Cry more than a baby."

"You would think Jane was a giant beast the way they cowered to her."

"She definitely has personality plus."

I smiled, taking a step closer. "Just like her owner."

I swore her eyes said she wanted to say something more, but she turned away and put the snorting dog in the kennel. "So, where are we headed anyway?"

"To a business meeting. Now come on, before we're late," I said, putting my hand on the small of her back.

She let out a small breath but didn't move my hand, my fingertips warming at the light touch of fabric meeting her skin.

When we stepped into the mild summer air, Grace headed for the parking garage. But I kept to the sidewalk and then turned to face her bewildered expression.

"Um, isn't that where your car's parked?" she asked, pointing at the entrance to the lot across the street.

"It is. But no need for it. We're just heading down Fleet." I pointed in the direction away from the parking garage.

She shook her head. "Didn't take you for much of a walker, especially after you just went out with Jane. You have a way of surprising me…"

I laughed. "Surprises can be a good thing."

"Sometimes." We stayed in a comfortable silence until we rounded the corner and the Temple Bar sign came into view.

"Is this meeting at Temple Bar? On a Saturday morning?" she asked, her eyes widening as she looked over the street ahead of us.

"Not the bar, but the market. Ever been? Not like the Portobello market in London, but they do have a few local food sellers and a book market." I glanced at her puzzled face.

"I've never been to the Portobello market, or this one. I don't know how either qualifies as work," she muttered.

I nodded, keeping my tone light as we walked in step down the cobblestone street. "I thought about what Lacey had said with her presentation. About using local sources and having them be a signature at the pubs."

Grace wrinkled her nose, and I laughed.

"That doesn't mean I'm stocking her wines in our pub, but maybe something else."

We headed underneath the large, white retractable umbrellas that created a roof canopy over the array of food booths.

My stomach growled, taking in the smell of freshly baked bread and melting chocolate.

Grace laughed. "I take it this is the booth we should stop

at? Thinking about switching up the soda bread?"

"I'm hungrier than I thought. Should have maybe eaten the croissants I brought this morning."

We approached the first booth we saw. I bought us a loaf of bread, some goat cheese, and two cups of coffee. Then we took our bag of goods and settled on a park bench.

"You know this still doesn't feel like any business meeting I've ever been to," she said before sipping her drink.

I scoffed as if she just said the most ridiculous thing, then dug into the bag of food. Though she was absolutely right.

"I really am here to test out the products. I needed the possible new head of purchasing with me to tell me if these were worth the investment."

She wrinkled her forehead, slightly turning her nose up. If we were playing poker, it would be a definite tell.

"I know that look on your face."

"I don't have a look," she quipped.

I smirked, putting my arm on the back of the bench as I faced her. "It's the one where you're rightfully pissed at me for bringing up the job. You won't say anything. But today, that's not going to happen."

I leaned in close, her lips slightly parting and letting out a soft breath. "So is this just about the job or are you going to tell me what else is giving you that look?"

She swallowed hard and looked down at her hands instead of meeting my gaze. "What do you want me to say? That this is all well and grand, you taking me to the market and pretending this is all for work. But we both know that your endgame is finding a wife and mine is to get another job in publishing or something to use my experience."

She blinked and then took a large gulp of her coffee as if she didn't mean to spit out the words and now was trying to take them back.

I waited until she looked at me again before I spoke.

"So that's your end goal here? Just working in publishing or editing? Not opening your own publishing house? Maybe even one in Dublin City Center?"

She looked at her cup, her shoulders falling. "If you must know, my pipe dream has always been to open my own boutique or small press. I'd love to be able to pick the stories I want to see published and help bring them from the author's head to the shelves."

"Then why aren't you doing this? Why come here with your mum and take the job with me?" I asked, genuinely curious.

"Many reasons."

"Such as?" I leaned forward, resting my arm on the back of the bench.

"I worked for one of the biggest publishers in Europe, hell, the world. Then they laid me off. I tried freelancing, but that fluctuates so much I couldn't depend on it for the bills. I applied for every job I could in publishing, but openings are few and far between. And don't get me started on my personal life."

I quirked an eyebrow, intrigued.

She shook her head. "I mean, not that it's anything crazy...just..."

Then she finally looked up. "You need a wife, Jack. I'm not a wife. I don't ever want to get married. And it's not because of a bad breakup or swearing off all men. It's... well...my parents' divorce was awful. I watched them fight it out for over a year and in the end my mum ended up with nothing, and that's the real reason we moved here. Though she'll never admit that."

I swallowed hard. Just as I was getting closer to her, she found a way to put a wall between us. One that should have stopped my need for her. But my racing heart had other ideas.

My hand crossed the small space between us and I took

hers in mine, interlacing our fingers.

She didn't push me away, but instead her eyes trailed from our interlocked hands, over the buttons of my shirt, and up to meet my gaze.

My chest tightened from the one little touch, and I sucked in a breath, trying to keep my composure. I focused on her light breathing and her warm fingers intertwined with mine. "I'm not about to pull out a ring and get down on one knee in the middle of the market. I'm just here with you, right now. That's it. Maybe you'll never marry and maybe one of the many lawyers I've had working on the will can find something to get my brothers and I out of this clause."

I brought her hand to my lips, brushing my mouth against her knuckles. Everything about this girl sparked new feelings inside of me. "But we can't worry about maybes."

I leaned in close.

"Pardon me, are you two almost done with this bench?" An old woman asked, staring at us and our barely touched food with her basket full of sweets.

*Well, I was just about to kiss my assistant.*

"Yes. We were just about to head to the book market," Grace said, quickly standing and scurrying toward a small row of tents with old books stacked as far as the eye could see.

Feck.

Well, if we were here for business, then that's what I would do. Make this about business.

I stopped where she stood in front of one of the tables, running her hands over the well-worn spines. "Did you read this book?"

I glanced at the faded green cover reading *The Jungle*.

"I did read this one and *Animal Farm* for our literature class."

She raised an eyebrow but a small smile still stayed on

her lips. "Really? I don't think I even read *Animal Farm*. Skimmed that one."

I laughed. "You missed a good one, from what I remember. Or was that the other one about the pig and the spider?"

"Please don't tell me you're getting *Animal Farm* confused with *Charlotte's Web*."

"There are a lot of similarities. Animals working together and learning literacy."

"You're stretching, but I would give you at least a C for effort," she said with a laugh.

"That's B worthy bullshite right there."

Turning toward the book seller, I stretched an arm out, getting his attention. "Sir. Do you think *Animal Farm* and *Charlotte's Web* are similar stories?"

The man adjusted his glasses. "Well, I guess on the surface they can appear that way. Fan of pig stories?"

"My grandda did have a few sows on his land when I was younger. Didn't think much of them."

The man nodded and moved to the other side of the booth where a few wooden crates were stacked. "I have these old photographs that we acquired from some of the Northside's deceased bookshops. Hold on. Let me find the one I'm thinking of."

He thumbed through a few yellowing photos in clear plastic cases before stopping on one and pulling it out. "Ah-ha, here's the one I was looking for."

I glanced at the black-and-white photo of a derelict farmhouse with a few sows and chickens begging an old woman for some scraps.

The image brought me back to my grandda's old stories he used to tell us. Much like when Grace and I went whiskey tasting, the old books and photographs brought back dozens of memories.

"I love the imagery in this. Kind of makes me wonder if that pig could be Snowball or Wilbur," Grace said, leaning into me, her silky brown hair brushing against my cheek.

Whatever shampoo she used smelled heavenly. My senses were filled with the sweet scent of coconut and I wanted to hold onto it and never let go.

Never? Feck.

"Thinking you want the photograph?" she asked, knocking me out of my scent-haze.

"Do you like it?" I asked, wanting her opinion. I trusted her completely. She never put on a front and always told me how it was.

"I like the imagery of it. That it shows the past of Dublin yet the future at the same time. Like those animals don't know that maybe that woman can't afford to keep feeding them, but she keeps trying. She keeps going to secure something more for them."

I didn't know if we were still talking about the photographs or if there was something deeper. A million thoughts swirled through my mind. I never thought talking books and photographs with a woman could make me smile this much. Or enjoy my time.

"How many more photographs do you have like this?" I asked the seller.

He whistled low then bent over the box, thumbing quickly through them, then looked skyward, counting on his hands. "Exactly like that, maybe half a dozen more. Pictures total, I have about fifty here and maybe like twenty more back at my flat. I think some of the other sellers might have some more, though, if you head down to the lad selling mystery novels in the blue tent."

I nodded. "I have one hundred new pubs going up in the U.S. within the next few years and could use more photos like these, so I'll take all that you have."

His eyes practically bugged out of his head as he adjusted his glasses. "All of them? I'd have to do some math and I'd need cash since I don't have a credit card reader."

I smiled. "Name your price and I can get to the first ATM or bank, and then point me to the next seller. And if you have any more books like this," I stopped and picked up the brightly colored copy of *Saorstait Eilean Handbook*. "I'll take those as well."

His head bobbed up and down. "Yes, sir."

"You don't need to do that," Grace whispered once the man was out of ear shot, thumbing through the books and putting them in an empty crate under his table.

"You were the one who brought up local sellers. What better way to honor Murphy's then use original artwork and pieces of Dublin's history?"

I glanced at her out of the corner of my eye, seeing her wide grin. The biggest I'd seen her have. "If this is all to impress me…"

I shook my head. "If I wanted to impress you, I would have probably just tried something like a fancy restaurant. We're just having some fun. Is that such a bad thing?"

She opened her mouth to say something but jumped when the seller cleared his throat. I turned toward him, and he stuffed his hands in his trouser pockets as he rambled off a price.

I nodded, pulling out my wallet and a few notes. "That should be about right. I have to grab my car and I'll be back to load them in the boot."

The man nodded, his wide eyes locked on the notes. "Yes, sir. I'll be here until we close at six."

"I'll be back before then," I said, shaking his hand before Grace and I headed toward the next stall.

"How did you get into literature and editing anyway?" I asked, my curiosity piqued.

Her face fell and my chest tightened, wishing I hadn't ruined that beautiful look on her face. "I think it was the only way my mother could figure out how to keep me busy when I was home. When I was actually at the house and not away at school or sent to stay with Granddad and Grandmum for the summer. She would get me stacks and stacks of books and I'd spend my entire holiday wrapped up in fictional worlds."

"She tried to get you something you cared about. It ended up being a career for you."

Her shoulder slumped. "Sorry that came off very brat-like of me, didn't it?"

"I've always been about work and ignored everything else. Made me terrible with my social life," I added, eyeing another table of worn vinyl records. It wasn't what we needed for the pub, but the brightly colored covers still caught my eye as we passed.

Her lips quirked, nose wrinkling. "I don't have much of a social life either. Work and Jane Pawsten. Well I guess if afternoon tea counts, as well. I've been putting that off now that I'm not staying at Granddad's. My family can be a bit interfering at times. I mean, I love them. But, you know."

"They mean well," I said, choosing my words carefully.

She straightened her shoulders. "I guess you can say that."

I took her hand in mine and interlaced our fingers. A shiver ran through me that I wasn't sure if it was from the blowing fan in the nearest booth or her touch.

She looked down, her cheeks a light crimson color as I turned toward her and stopped.

Feck, she was beautiful. And smart. And witty. The first woman who, in a long time, I could see more than a night with.

*What was I thinking?*

This was Grace I was talking about.

A family friend. My brother's best mate. And now my assistant.

Yet the more I thought about pushing myself away, the harder I pulled myself forward.

I smiled. "Let's pick out some more photographs. Then we can stop by the butcher and grab a bone for Jane Pawsten before we head back to your flat."

I brushed my thumb along her knuckles and watched the shiver run through her. "While we meet some more of the vendors, you can tell me what else I've missed all of these years of not spending time with you."

She let out a deep breath. "Not much to say, really. It'll be a short convo and there's a lot of market left."

"How did you happen to end up with the little furball then? Seems like she's quite a story herself," I asked.

A look of glee returned to her face. "She actually started out as my grandmum's. She learned how to use the internet and went on a spending spree. Aside from a new sofa set and BMW, she also ordered a set of Brussels Griffon puppies."

I couldn't help the laugh that escaped my lips, making my cheeks hurt from smiling this much. I couldn't remember the last time I'd laughed, grinned, or enjoyed someone's company like with Grace. "Really?"

She laughed, nodding. "I can't even make this up. When my mum found out, of course, she had to find a place for the puppies to go since she couldn't return them. I wound up going home with a little brown bundle who hasn't left my side the past few years."

"She is a grand dog."

I turned with her, walking the path in front of the book stalls. "She's a little shite is what she is, but I'm attached to that little shite. I couldn't imagine my life without her."

As we continued on, I found myself staring at this beautiful woman. Even though we'd only been reacquainted for a short while, just like with the dog, I couldn't imagine my life without her. I wanted to spend nights curled up on the couch with her and the little dog. Waking up to feast on this beautiful woman's skin before work.

I had to find a wife. She didn't want to be one.

Instead of running, I walked with her hand in hand through the market.

"Stop at this one?" I asked, pointing at the booth full of worn out romance novels.

She laughed. "I guess if you want to add some Highlander romance to the pubs it could really spice things up."

I laughed. "Never read one. Think you can give me the Cliff's Notes?"

She huffed but the grin broadened on her face. "I knew you didn't actually read the books."

"Only the good ones. The others, I'll have you tell me about."

She picked up one of the books from the table with a man and woman embraced on a ship. "Want me to read you the synopsis on this one?"

I smiled, thinking I could listen to this woman read me the phone book. "That would be grand."

# Chapter Thirteen

GRACE

I loved reading because it gave me an escape from the real world, especially romance novels. The men were usually gentlemen, even the bad boys, who could bring a girl to their knees.

Even though I still wasn't sure that books were his thing, Jack talked literature with me.

I found that sweet. I never thought of him as a guy who would do something like that. He was so businesslike.

This was the softer side of Jack. As we went through the market, he spoke with every vendor like they were an old friend, letting them explain the photographs or Celtic books.

Damn he was sexy when he pushed his hair back and laughed as he talked to the sellers.

*What the hell was wrong with me?*

I couldn't be falling for my boss. Or Sean's brother.

Guilt riddled me even more about the entire situation when I got a text from Sean.

Sean: *What's up? Wanna grab a bite after practice today?*

Me: *I would, but I'm working today. I don't know for how long.*

Sean: *Work? On a Saturday? Do I need to talk to Jack about this?*

Me: *No. It's totally fine. I'll message you later, though.*

"That my brother?" Jack asked.

"No. Just checking my email," I said quickly, tucking my phone back into my pocket.

"Funny, because he just messaged me asking what I was doing keeping you at work on a Saturday morning."

"Blast," I muttered.

After we loaded the last of the boxes in the back of his car, he turned toward me. "I have to take these to Murphy's. Then you can get back to Sean so he doesn't think I have you locked in a dungeon or something."

His lips quirked, flashing those damn dimples. "But I don't want you to give Jane that bone without me. I want to see how excited she gets for it."

I wanted to lean forward and kiss those dimples. "I think you like my dog more than me."

"I like you, Grace. Not for your dog or because you're a family friend. But because of who you are. All those books and you didn't get yourself a single one."

"I didn't need another book," I muttered, trying to change the subject and not think that I could be equally falling for this man.

He smiled, opening the door and pulling out a small

plastic sack on top of the box, handing it to me. "I'll just keep these for myself then."

"You did not buy those for me," I gasped, looking into the sack to see a few old paperbacks looking back at me. He'd been paying attention. I had perused all of these, wishing I could spare some money for them, but thought it would be too frivolous.

"Thank you, Jack. You didn't have to, and I swear I'll pay you back every penny for this and Jane's bills."

Though I didn't know how I'd ever get the money for that.

"Don't worry about any of it. The books are a gift. You've been doing great work at the office."

I'm not sure I could handle him being so nice.

I let out a deep breath, my shoulders falling.

"You okay?" he asked with a frown.

I nodded. "Yeah, just all day in the sun, I guess. Kind of have a stomach ache."

I winced for good measure.

"I'll get you home." Deep down I knew I should just say goodbye, but my heart wasn't listening.

"Do you still want to come up and give Janey her bone?"

"Definitely."

I laughed. "I'm sure you're going to be her favorite after you give it to her."

He took my hand. I should have let go and told him I didn't want to go there. That I shouldn't have even held onto him at the market. But once our fingers intertwined, all resolve left me and I guided him up the stairs to my flat.

As soon as we opened the door, Jane Pawsten whined from her cage.

"I'm coming girl," I said as we walked to her little crate.

I released his hand and, as soon as I opened the door, she bolted out and right into Jack's arms. "Hey, girl, good to see you missed me."

She snorted, rubbing her face in his trouser pockets which made Jack laugh. "Ah, I take it you smell the surprise I got for you."

"Wait," I yelled, grabbing onto his hand and ignoring the jolt every time my fingers grazed his.

"Yes?" he asked, slowly titlting his head.

I grabbed Jane's leash from the rack on the wall. "I need to walk her first. She's been inside all day and if she gets too excited, she'll piss all over the floor."

He nodded, his lips forming a thin line that I wasn't sure if it meant he was disappointed or just deep in thought. "Then I guess we're going on a walk."

"We?" I asked.

"Unless you plan on kicking me out, I want to see if you have this dog mastered to not chase after every leaf."

I shook my head but my heart still warmed at the thought.

As much as I should have probably ran and kicked the guy out right there or made excuses, instead I put Jane's leash on and took Jack's hand, leading him out of the flat with me.

Maybe it was the summer air, or the fact that Jack laughed as much as I did, watching my little dog think she was tough stuff by barking at every other passing puppy, but I was starting to see the man before me in a different light.

One that I was desperately trying to avoid but couldn't.

Once we got back to my flat and let Janey go to her water bowl, I thought this was the time I could tell him it was time for the day to end.

But I didn't want to. In this moment I could forget everything and give in to what I wanted with this sweet, caring man. Throw caution to the wind and just kiss him.

So instead, I did what any person would do and offered food instead of making out. "You know it's been a while since we've eaten and its past lunch. There aren't many delivery places around here, but I could get Chinese if you're hungry."

"I can order it," he said, already pulling out his phone. "Should I order rice for Jane as well?"

Blast, why did he have to flash those damn dimples and bring up my dog?

"Yeah. Plain white, though. And I'll grab some notes from my pocketbook," I said, mentally calculating how much I actually had in my wallet.

But Jack waved me off and ordered for both of us and the dog.

When the order arrived, we were in the middle of a game of tug of war with Jane and I almost frowned, not wanting this to be another sign that the day needed to end. That we shouldn't be getting comfortable.

"Do you have a lot of takeaway locations in London? From my trips to America it seems like they're on every corner. Something Connor and Fallon still won't stop talking about," Jack said, plating us each a portion of sesame chicken and rice. Then, of course, getting Janey a plate.

"Yes, but nothing like America. Did you know they have pizza trattoria's that are open and deliver until four in the morning?" I asked, taking my plate as Jack sat down next to me in at the little table by the window.

He nodded. "Connor told me about those. He and Fallon seemed to bond over all things American."

I took a bite of my food, trying not to think about how I was also slowly forming a tie with Sean's older brother. Even so much that I told Sean I had dinner plans with a friend from work. He didn't need to know that friend was Jack.

"Late night food would have been grand in uni, hell even when we were at Le Instuit. Could you imagine if we could order pizza in the middle of the night? The headmaster would have had a fit," I said, shaking my head.

Jack laughed. "I could just see him now, and that forehead vein popping as he stood in his office, yelling on and on about handing out pepperoni demerits."

"Pepperoni demerits?" I asked with a laugh.

"Would you prefer cheese expulsion?"

I wrinkled my nose but couldn't wipe the smile off my face. "That sounds even worse."

He tilted his head back and laughed, his whole body shaking. "Okay. You're right about that one."

"That sounds like some of the items I've had to cut out of the romance novels I've worked on lately. One woman had that the hero growled no less than twenty times and even used the phrase 'heaving bosom.'"

Jack erupted in laughter, covering his mouth as he cleared his throat before speaking again. "I thought that was just a myth and no one actually wrote like that."

"Well, no one does. Or talks like that. Thus, I told her she could never utter that phrase again and only got two 'he growled' per book."

"Growling and bosoms. Seems like you have your hands full with editing. And yet you left the freelance work to come to Murphy's. Maybe I'll sneak some of those in memos and see if you notice." He nodded and a hint of a smile played on his lips.

I shook my head. "What if I didn't catch those?"

He laughed. "Well, you're pretty damn good at your job, so I know you would unless you were doing it out of spite. Then I'd have to explain to the board why all of a sudden our franchise owners growl and have heaving bosoms."

I covered my mouth to hide an unladylike snort that I was sure would have come out of my mouth.

But he didn't comment on that and just continued with stories, making me laugh more than I had in ages while we finished up our dinner and then cleaned up.

As he slowly went to the door, I didn't want him to leave, but also didn't want to appear desperate.

"Oh. Almost forgot this," he said, pulling out the bone from his pocket and kneeling down to the whining dog at his feet.

She didn't want him to leave either but forgot all about her protesting when he gave her the little treat. She happily took it then pranced over to her bed near the couch, chomping down on it.

"I need to head out now. Need to get some stuff together for contacting the sellers on Monday," Jack said, his gaze on the dog instead of meeting mine.

I nodded. "Oh. Yeah. I understand."

I didn't know if this situation warranted a hug, or a handshake, or what. But, without thinking, I stood up straighter and pressed my lips to his for a light goodbye kiss.

But his touch was anything but light as his arms wrapped around my waist and I melted against him.

I told myself I couldn't get too close. That I had to ignore how blasted sweet the man had been to all of the sellers and to me and Janey.

But instead I gasped when his tongue met mine, his mouth savoring me as if he couldn't get enough, and his hands roamed to my hips.

I tried to protest, but my brain couldn't process the words. I could only moan as he trailed his mouth down my neck. Everything inside of me said I should be saying "no," but when I opened my mouth only breathless whispers escaped.

I ran my hands through his hair, down his neck, wanting to ingrain every part of him in my memory. My body moved without conscious effort, as I fisted his shirt, pulling him backward toward the living room.

*Mo gra*," he whispered, his lips by my ear as I pulled him down to the couch. He hovered over me as I leaned back, relishing the feel of his warm mouth on my neck, trailing to my collarbone and back up.

I worked the buttons of his shirt; my hands landed on his bare chest, roaming wherever I could reach as we kissed. As fine a specimen as the man was in his tailored suits, shirtless Jack was reminiscent of a Greek God. I ran my hands over every dip and curve of his hard chest and abs, committing his form to memory.

Soon he would be gone and this moment I would have to pretend didn't exist. But while I had him above me, I wanted to imbed every part of this man into my memory.

Not the arsehole from school or my boss or my best mate's brother. But the sexy man who made me weak in the knees and I couldn't get enough of.

His fingers continued their dance, skirting along the edges of my thighs and when his thumb moved between us, swiping along my damp panties, I gasped, pressing deeper into him as our kisses drowned out my moan.

It had been so long since any man had touched me like this. Even so, there was never this slow buildup in my chest either. The one that was tying me to Jack. The man I shouldn't hbe falling for when he needed a wife.

But with each kiss and moan, I was becoming more and more attached to him. Walking away from him just wasn't going to happen.

He may need something more than me, but I had to give in to what my pounding heart and every fiber of my body was aching for.

I gently broke the kiss, my eyes locked on his as I peeled off my dress and sweater.

I should have been embarrassed that I was lying there in my strapless bra that barely contained my chest or that I was wearing a tiny swatch of fabric for undies.

But the way Jack's eyes roamed over me, biting his bottom lip before he looked back into my eyes, had my entire body on fire.

"You're so fecking beautiful," he murmured, his fingers trailing down my collarbone and over the swell of my breasts before his lips were back on mine, his kisses hungry with need.

No one had ever called me beautiful. I'd never heard a man speak to me in that breathy, husky tone that curled my toes.

"You know it isn't fair that you're still dressed." I whimpered as he pressed his lips to my neck.

What was I saying?

I should have listened to my head and not gotten wrapped up in this man, but my heart and aching core were saying so much more.

"I'm not here to shag you, *mo gra*. Right now, I'm just enjoying the feel of you," he whispered, his lips trailing down my collar bone again and then continuing their way down the dips and curves of my body.

His hot breath landed on my panties and I arched my back without thinking, willing him to continue.

But there was no controlling a man like Jack Murphy, and instead of putting his hand or mouth exactly where I wanted him to, his lips trailed to the apex of my thighs, nuzzling the sensitive nerves of my skin.

Blast, this man knew just how to turn a woman on.

But more than being a puddle of goo at his touch, he was becoming a part of me. A part of me I wanted to keep.

I ran my hands through his hair again, tousling the usually meticulously styled locks. He rested his chin on my thigh, looking up at me with hooded blue eyes.

"Ever since I first saw you at the gala, I've been dying to savor you."

"So this is about my looks then?" I asked in a whisper, wanting to kick myself for blurting that out.

"I think we both know it's more than that," he murmured.

His mischievous eyes stayed on mine as he placed a soft kiss on my thigh. "You're smart."

Another kiss. "Witty."

"Sexy."

Another kiss.

And with that, any resolve I had was completely gone. My body vibrated with need. Screw inheritance clauses and forced marriages. All I could think about was him touching me and teetering on the brink of orgasm just from a few kisses.

"Jack...don't make me beg...I want you." I barely got the words out before his mouth was back on mine. I moaned into his mouth as our tongues tangled together.

The rest of our clothes seemed to melt away, coming off piece by piece as we kissed and explored each other's bodies.

As if we had just made a silent agreement, he pulled a foil packet out of his trousers and slipped it over his impressive length before guiding himself inside me.

I let out a low moan, relishing each exquisite inch.

"You feel so feckin good, *mi stolin*," he murmured, rocking his body against mine.

The accent alone was enough to make my body hum. Combined with his hard body and the way he moved, every part of me sang.

Was there anything this man wasn't good at?

We moved slowly in a rhythm, him pulling completely out of me, then slamming back in, each time making me gasp and throw my head back in ecstasy.

"Ah," I moaned. Everything I'd tried to keep down for so long boiled to the surface. Whether we moved fast or slow, every inch of him filled me, and a new sense of pleasure coursed through me.

There was nothing else at that moment. Just Jack and me.

Gripping his shoulders, I rode out the waves of pleasure

coursing through me, a moment that made me see stars and electricity pulse through my body.

His lips were back on mine, savoring me. This moment. Unspoken words between us.

He moaned into my mouth as he rocked into me, his heavy breathing meeting the rapid beat of my own heart as he shuddered, laying his rock-hard body against mine.

We kissed a few minutes longer, still connected, his body covering mine. Then he gazed up at me, pushing a fallen strand of hair behind my ear and whispered, "I've been waiting a long time for that."

"Me too," I admitted in a whisper. I knew that we were playing a very dangerous game. And at the end of the day, I wasn't sure either of us would win.

# Chapter Fourteen

## JACK

I wanted to fall asleep with Grace in my arms. To wake her up with my cock buried deep inside of her so she would only think of me and smell me on her skin for days.

How could I think like that? My priority was the company. *A wife.*

Jane interrupted my thoughts, pawing at the bed, whimpering as she stared up at us with beady black eyes.

"I should probably get her a water refill. I think she downed that bone," Grace whispered.

Lifting my head, I looked into Grace's eyes, but she kept her stare downward. This was more than just about the dog. "Do you really need to get her some water or are you just saying that so you can kick me out of your bed?"

She got up slowly, grabbing her dress and sliding it on over her head before she grabbed the dog's bowl, filling it with water.

"Do you want the truth or a lie?"

I wasn't sure.

"Never lie, it's not who you are."

My brothers would surely kill me if they knew what I was doing.

But the thought of all of this going south, for her, for the company, riddled my stomach with guilt.

"I don't regret this. And I know what you need is a wife," she murmured. "So it's really not something we should repeat."

The air *whooshed* from my lungs.

I didn't know if I could change her mind.

The part of me that wanted what was best for the company was yelling at my brain that I needed to end this now.

But my heart, the blasted thing, wasn't going to listen.

I leaned in and kissed her slowly. "Okay."

"Okay?" she asked hestitantly, wincing slightly.

"Okay. We won't talk marriage. We won't talk anything further than this moment."

*For now.*

• • •

I didn't see Grace on Sunday, though I ached to see her. To have her again. I couldn't get the damn woman out of my head.

On my way to the office on Monday morning, I spotted a stand selling different candies and one caught my eye. Magic Stars. I didn't spend much time with Grace in our school days, but I did remember that she had Magic Stars in her bag when she came for the summers. This was ingrained in my memory since most of the other girls I knew wouldn't be caught dead with sweets.

When I got to the office, Grace was on the phone and barely looked up from the computer. But there was something different about her today. Instead of the stiff white oxfords and long black skirts that she tended to wear at the office, she wore a light floral dress that I remembered from the meeting at the café.

Her face also had more color, and that was probably because she had finally been thoroughly shagged. The thought of her spread across that desk with my cock buried deep inside her flashed across my mind. I had to get a grip, especially at the office.

I did the gentlemanly thing, placing the sweets and coffee on her desk and whispering, "Come see me in my office when you're done."

She nodded, her gaze briefly flitting to mine before she returned to her call.

I smiled and then closed the door behind me.

I'd barely opened my emails and taken my first sip of coffee when a knock came at the door.

"Why did you put these on my desk?" she asked.

I frowned. "If my memory serves me, you loved those when we were younger. I may not have recognized you without the curly hair and braces, but I do remember a little bit of the girl who always carried these sweets."

Her shoulders slumped. "These candy bars were half the reason girls gave me hell in school. I acted like I didn't give a rip, but when every twig bitch starts making comments during fencing, it takes a toll."

Shite. I thought I was doing something right, now I was really fecking it up. My shoulders tensed and my jaw clenched.

Standing from my desk, I rounded the corner and put a gentle hand on her shoulder. "I'm sorry. I didn't know—"

"You really had no idea?" she asked softly.

I shook my head. "None whatsoever. I just thought you liked them. I saw them on my walk in and thought of you."

She sighed. "Why do you have to be so nice to me? It

makes it hard not to like you."

I laughed. "Would you rather I be a jerk? I could tell you that the chocolate bar is actually for me and I expected you to bring it when I got hungry."

She put her hands on her hips, trying to appear tough, but her body shook as she kept her mouth in a thin line, trying not to laugh.

"Really?"

I shook my head, unable to hold back my own laugh. "No. But that was the most arseholish thing I could think of at the moment."

She sighed, dropping her arms and walking closer, closing the space between us before she leaned against the desk. "You're a right pain in the arse."

"You don't want me to boss you around or be nice. So maybe I'll just stop talking. How about if I do this instead?" I murmured, leaning into her neck and trailing my lips along her skin.

She sighed, tilting her head to the side, so I could nip and suck the sensitive flesh.

Feck she smelled amazing, her skin even tasted like the sweet scent of vanilla and coffee. I could savor her inch by inch if she'd let me.

"We probably shouldn't be doing this. But dammit, don't stop either," she whispered, but her shaky words didn't match her body leaning into me and her hands gripping my biceps.

I laughed slightly before my fingers went to her beautiful arse, and I lifted her off the ground and pushed her onto the desk, her skirt rising with her. Pushing between her thighs, the heat of her core pressed against my already aching dick. I moaned as her hands fisted my hair and sweet little gasps vibrated her body.

I'd never had a woman in my office like this, never wanted to take the chance on this fantasy. Until her.

"I don't have any meetings until later this morning and I can lock the door," I murmured, sliding my hand up her skirt to her bare thigh, my gaze staying on her gorgeous brown eyes.

She nodded slightly. "Okay."

Quickly I locked the door then went back to her. My lips immediately tangled with hers again and my hand inched up her thigh.

She spread her legs, pulling me against her as I pushed aside the damp material of her panties, running my thumb along her center.

Watching her body writhe around me was exquisite torture. I'd never be able to look at my desk the same way knowing I watched her come apart on it.

I didn't hear the doorknob wiggling. But I did hear Connor loud and clear as he pounded on the door and yelled about why I would need a lock.

Blast, the cock block.

"We can pretend we aren't here," I whispered, kissing the delicate curve of her neck.

"I know you're in there, and Grace, too. You two better not be in the whiskey without me."

Feck.

I pulled back from Grace as she slowly slid off the desk with a frown.

"I hope the entire office didn't hear that," she whispered, grabbing some random papers off the desk and carrying them toward the door. I followed her.

"I'll make sure any rumors are squashed immediately," I said, placing a light kiss on her cheek.

She nodded but her eyes stayed downward as I opened the door.

I glared at my brother.

Grace kept her head down as she headed toward her

desk, her face scarlet. "I'll get these typed up for you right away, Mr. Murphy."

Connor smiled, then followed me into the office, closed the door behind us, and raised his eyebrows. "What just happened? Why was her face so red? Is there something more than whiskey that I need to know about?"

"It's none of your business. We were just discussing some personal matters. And why the hell did you need to pull that scene?" I glowered.

He laughed, shaking his head. "No one was at their desks yet and I knew that would get you off your arse."

"You're a right *pain* in the arse, you know that?"

"Speaking of pains in the arse… I thought you were one to Grace but seeing her scarlet when she walked out of here tells me something else. Is there something going on you want to tell me about? A new sister-in-law in the works?"

I shook my head. It was too soon to be thinking about things like marrying Grace when we were just getting reacquainted. But that didn't stop my pulse from racing when the idea was mentioned. "It's not like that."

"Then what is it? Are you trying to use her to make Lacey jealous?" he asked, crossing his arms over his chest.

I frowned. Connor had a way of pushing every single one of my buttons and knew it. "Are you mad? Why would I give a shite what Lacey thinks?"

Is that what Grace thought? Did she think I still had some lingering feelings for the bird?

"Grace, you look flustered, please tell me you aren't working too hard," Sean's voice carried into the room as he threw the door open. He had one tattooed hand on the handle with his head thrown back in Grace's direction.

"No, work's fine. I just choked on my coffee a bit," she sputtered, her brown waves the only thing I could see over my youngest brother's massive biceps.

Sean entered the room after saying his goodbyes to Grace and Fallon then shut the door, standing between Connor and me.

He ran his fingers through the scruff of his beard and looked between us. "Why do you two look like someone just caught you pissing in the holy water?"

Connor threw his arms in the air. "You take a dare one time in school, and that's what you're known for forever."

Sean grinned.

I sat down at my desk. I could still smell Grace on me.

I wasn't complaining.

"Is there a reason you two are here unannounced?" I asked, trying to clear my mind.

"Well, since you've been ignoring her calls, Lacey has been messaging me about the Poppy Wines deal," Connor said, ambling toward my desk before propping himself on the edge.

"Never liked Lacey. She was always a bitch, not just to me but to Grace as well. For that alone, I'd say 'feck her' on the deal. Though I did hear Grace took the piss outta her during the meeting. I wish I could have seen that," Sean said with a laugh, plopping in the leather chair across from me with a loud *thud*.

Shaking my head, I let out a breath. "Let's say 'feck it' with the Poppy deal. No matter what they're offering. We don't need their wines. I looked over Grace's points from the meeting and she's right."

Sean scowled, crossing his arms over his chest. "Since when do you take this much advice from an assistant?"

"Probably since he's been crushing on the bird," Connor said, smacking the wooden surface next to him.

Sean's eyes went from curious to menacing, the dark black of his pupils taking over his entire eye. He stood up, his fists clenched tightly at his side. "You and Grace? I thought you two hated each other?"

"Sometimes things change. We all have grown up. Grace is brilliant, funny, and bloody hell, I do really like her." My ears burned, all the hair on the back of my neck standing on end. I'd never said my feelings out loud for her and admitting anything caused a flutter in my chest like never before.

"So why aren't you getting down on your knees, or well one knee?" Connor asked.

"It's not like that with us, and you can't just propose to a girl you just met." I scoffed.

He shook his head. "First off, you've known her since we were kids and, second, if it's real and there's a ticking time clock of an inheritance clause, you can."

"You're absolutely mad, has anyone ever told you that?" I asked.

"All the time." He laughed.

"Are you really that into Grace?" Sean asked slowly, his dark eyes locked in a glare.

"I'm not saying I'm going to propose right now, but I have been spending more time with her. I really was a shite when we were younger, and I guess I'm trying to make up for that now."

Sean shook his head. "I never thought I'd see her with you."

"And who did you expect her with, you?" I asked, wondering what I would do if my little brother did say he had feelings for her.

He pressed his fingers to the bridge of his nose and let out a deep breath. "No. I never saw her like that. I always thought she'd find someone, and I'd be there to give the guy shite and probably hate him. But thinking of you with her...well..."

"Yes?" I asked, leaning forward.

He blew out a large breath, his barrel of a chest puffing beneath his shirt. "I don't know. It's strange. You're so into your work and with the inheritance clause… What if this all comes down and crashes and burns? Then where does that leave us? Without the company? With her family hating us?"

"I don't want that to happen either. You have to believe me, I've thought the same things, but I also can't stay away. I've tried, believe me, but I keep going back. She's everything I didn't know I wanted or needed at the same time."

Connor laughed. "Sounds like someone's getting ready to propose and now we just need to find a girl for Sean. Still flirting with Fallon's American friend via text?"

He replied by shaking his head. "You're all mad—you know that? I came here to talk business and now I'm probably going to be late for practice because you two want to gossip about girls."

He stood up straighter, his full height looming. "Jack. If you really are going to start something with Grace, make sure you finish it."

"Don't worry, Sean, I'm not a quitter, and I'll be good to her."

For however long we can make whatever this is last.

"You'd better," he grumbled. "But I'm not saying I like this idea of the two of you together."

He ran his hand down his face, his fingers getting twisted in his beard. "Don't feck this up, okay? Grace is one of my best mates and I don't know what I'd do if you hurt her."

I nodded. "I promise. Right now, we are just seeing where this goes."

She wanted nothing to do with marriage and had told me that, multiple times.

I needed a wife and not a fling, or whatever this was.

But I couldn't stop now.

And this would either be the biggest mistake I ever made, or the best.

# Chapter Fifteen

Blasted Jack Murphy.

When Sean came into the office I was even more on edge, wondering if the fact I slept with his brother was obvious and written on my face.

This entire situation was complicated and I was glad Jack was in meetings all day.

By the time I got home with Jane Pawsten, I was more than ready to change and go for our nightly walk after dinner.

What I didn't expect was my phone to buzz in the middle of my playlist.

Pulling the device out of my pocket, I couldn't help the grin on my face when I saw the message.

Blast. What was happening to me?

Jack: *Finally out of meetings and about to grab a bite. Join me?*

I sighed even though he couldn't hear me. I'd love to sit

across the table from him, share food, drinks, and see where we ended up.

But us together was a one-time thing. Two if you counted his office. No. I couldn't lead him on. Not when he needed a wife to keep his company.

Me: *Sorry, already ate and taking Jane Pawsten for a walk.*

*Jack: I can join the two of you.*

Warning bells buzzed in my head but instead of following them, I texted back.

Me: *If you insist. We'll meet you in front of the Murphy gates.*

My heart sped up with each step and not just because I swore Janey trotted faster as soon as she knew we were headed toward the building.

Jack leaned against one of the posts, a broad smile on his face as soon as we approached.

She barked happily, bouncing on his feet as soon as we were close enough.

"Jane Pawsten, the happiest girl in the world," he said with a laugh, bending down and scratching behind her ears.

He looked up at me before slowly standing. "And hello to you, too."

"You sure you have the footwear for a walk?" I blurted, trying to focus on his leather shoes and blue trousers instead of his gorgeous face

"Are we heading for the Boston marathon or to the park?" He reached into his pocket, pulling out a small tennis ball, tossing it once in the air and catching it.

Janey stood on her hind legs, barking up at the little green thing flying through the air.

I laughed, putting my hand to my chest, trying to ignore the way my whole body warmed for this little gesture. "When did you get a ball?"

He laughed. "Used to play a lot of tennis in uni and found this in one of the drawers in the office. Her mouth is too small to fetch it, but at least she'll have fun chasing it."

"Let's try it out," I said with a smile as we walked together toward one of the parks, Janey prancing happily between us.

I shouldn't have gotten so close to him, but with each step it was as if a weight had been lifted off my shoulders. Being myself and having a good time with him was easy.

Once we got to an area of green space, Jack tossed the ball a few meters and Jane happily chased after it, barking when she couldn't pick it up in her mouth. But she was brilliant. She found a way to kick it back with her front paws like a futball.

"Told you she'd get it," Jack said with a laugh, grabbing the little green ball from the dog who looked up at him with her tail wagging.

He tossed the ball again; Jane chased after it.

"She really likes that. I should maybe invest in some tennis balls, then she wouldn't try to eat Grandmum's plants," I said, watching her kick the ball back to us.

"I did some research the other day about dogs and their boredom habits. It may be hard for Jane sitting all day at your grandparents' or in her crate."

"Way to lay the guilt trip on," I muttered, watching the dog instead of what I assumed would be a harsh look from Jack.

He laughed. "Not a guilt trip, but I can spend my lunch with her, tossing the ball to burn off some steam of my own. And you can see about enrolling her in a doggy daycare. I heard those are a big thing now."

Before I could respond he nodded to himself. "You know what? I'll make a call tomorrow. See if we can get her enrolled in one down the block. We can put it on the Murphy's card and see if it's something we can do for all employees eventually. There are the legalities with daycare and children, but maybe at least a discount program for dogs and kids alike."

I didn't know what he was getting at but there was a new shifting feeling in my chest. Not just talking about taking care of my dog, but now he was bringing up kids? What was this all really about?

"I can't ask you to do that for her or me. I'll look into doggy daycares myself," I stammered.

I didn't want to tell him that there was also no way I could afford doggy daycare. Sure, I was living rent-free, but my first paycheck was already going back to my grandparents for the clothes and Jack for the vet bills, even though they were trying to refuse it. An extra twenty euros a day on doggy daycare would add to the growing list of bills.

"You didn't have to ask. I want to do it." I finally looked up to see his broad smile before he threw the ball again.

"You want to spend time with my dog?" I asked carefully, swallowing the lump in my throat.

*And me?*

"I'm cooped up in the office all day and could use a break in the afternoon. Fresh air helps me think. And besides…" He shot me a wink. "I can spend time with her owner, too."

Right there I should have reiterated that I never wanted to get married. That spending time with my dog wasn't going to change that.

But it wasn't true.

I really liked him. The way he played with Janey and took care of us was more than anyone had ever done before. My parents' relationship didn't work because they had nothing in common. I never saw them spend time together outside of sitting at the dinner table or at the conference table during their divorce fights.

"Were you able to eat anything before you met up with us? I don't want to keep you from dinner," I said, blurting the first thing I could to interrupt my nagging thoughts.

"I can grab something later," he replied.

I knew I should've listen to my head but my heart ruled out, knowing exactly what happened last time we shared a meal at my place. "I'm not the best cook in the world, but I can make a mean toastie with crisps."

He grinned, those dimples flashing and my stomach warmed. "I'll grab something on the way home."

"I want to. Can I please make you a sandwich and crisps?"

He laughed. "Fine. If you insist."

After a few more tosses of the ball, we went back to my flat where Janey gulped down a bowl of water then laid on the floor snoring, while I made a sandwich for Jack and tea for both of us.

"Best grilled cheese I've ever had," Jack said with a grin as I took the seat next to him at the small table.

"It's some of that brown bread and farmhouse cheese from the market. Nothing too fancy, but it's good." I shrugged nonchalantly, taking a sip of my tea.

Truth was, no one ever complimented me on much, especially not my food. Even if it was just toasties.

"This is why you'd be great in purchasing. You find the best our local market has to offer and put it together. I'll contact them to see if they're interested in at least supplying to the local pubs."

"Really?" I asked, trying to contain my excitement. I'd worked in publishing for years and had my senior editors tell me my stuff was good, but never make more of an effort past that.

Not that I needed the praise, but when it came from Jack, my heart that was already beating rapidly went at full speed.

"Yeah. Your opinion matters to me." His hand went to

my knee and I should have swatted him away but instead I put my hand on his, squeezing it lightly.

He put his sandwich down, leaning in. "Not just in the company, *mo gra*, but your opinion of me matters, too. What can I do to convince you I'm not the same gobshite I was when we were younger?"

"You already have," I whispered, pressing my lips to his and letting the world melt away around us.

• • •

I wanted to hate Jack Murphy.

But I couldn't.

When he spoke sweetly and kissed me, all resolve melted.

My nights after work were spent with him and Jane at the park, then dinner and falling into bed together. Finally, I was connected with someone else, physically and mentally.

But guilt ached inside me.

Now that there was something more brewing, I couldn't help but think on my mum's words. And my own.

What if Jack and I really started dating? Then would she and Grandmum only assume it was to dupe him into falling for me and getting the company? They knew how I felt about marriage and it was only a matter of time before Jack realized that this wouldn't end where he wanted it to.

By then it might be too late.

It would not only break me, but he could lose the company.

I could have stayed in bed, going over the scenarios that wounded my heart. But Jane yapped from the pillow next to me, alerting me I'd better feed her or she'd never shut up.

Once I let the dog out and poured her kibble, I looked at my phone and saw a missed email and call. It was Saturday, and Jack had planned another "business trip" as he called it to the market to meet with the bread seller.

I was pretty sure it was code for talking to the seller for five minutes then shagging. But he really did seem to be excited about the prospect of more local products in the pub, even showing off the photos he purchased to the board members whenever one of them stopped in.

Carolyn, my former editor, sent the email that *pinged* on my phone. I opened it and had barely read the "greetings" line when my former colleague, Sarah, called.

"Hello?" I answered, adrenaline coursing through me. I didn't get through the entire email but the terms *new line* and *need an editor* jumped out at me.

"Why did it take you so long to answer?" Sarah got right to the point. I guess that's why she was one of the few people I got along within the office. But I never considered us phone friends. I didn't even remember I had her number in my contacts.

"It's Saturday. I just woke up." I turned on the kettle. Jack would probably bring coffee, or we'd get some at the market, but I loved a morning cuppa.

"Did you get the email from Carolyn?"

"Uh-huh. I just saw it," I said, trying to hide the trepidation in my voice. What if she was calling to tell me that she accepted an offer as senior editor and wanted to make me her assistant?

"As you know, I've got a lot on my plate here. Especially since they let so many people go."

"Right."

"Carolyn approached me about the new line and asked if I knew anyone who might be interested in the senior editor position. I thought of you. I don't know what you're up to these days, but it's a hell of an opportunity. Way better pay, too."

"Oh. Wow." Everything swirled in my head, my heart

pounding in my ears. This was the phone call I'd been waiting for since the day I was laid off. I should be jumping for joy, but instead, something else tugged at my heartstrings.

No...someone.

"Wow, this is...this is not what I expected," I said, trying to come up with the right words.

"I would've thought you'd be over the moon about this. But you sound like I just yelled at your dog," she said, annoyance ringing in her voice.

"No. I'm just. Well, I'm in shock is all."

She laughed. "Okay. I get that. But you'd better email Carolyn back ASAP, and hopefully, I'll see you back in the office next week."

"Thanks. I will," I said, my brain still in a fog as we exchanged a few niceties before I disconnected the call.

It was everything I'd dreamed—running my own line with a successful publisher.

The only problem with all of this was that it left Jack and Ireland out of the equation. The job was in London. No virtual position.

The answer should have been easy. I should have been able to say "yes" to this dream job. Not seriously thinking about staying at Murphy's Pub and with Jack.

Yet there I stood, staring at my phone, not noticing I was crying until the tears hit my lip.

I never cried over a man. Not one I dated and not my father when he left after the divorce was final. So why now?

Sighing, I decided to hop in the shower and get ready for the day. I tried to put everything about the job in the back of my mind and focus on my day with Jack.

Our time was coming to an end.

• • •

"I saw a gourmet dog treat booth that we'll need to check out," Jack said as we walked through the market.

We'd been quiet, but it had not been an uncomfortable silence. There was something about him that made it easy to say nothing at all with either of us thinking something was wrong.

But something was very wrong. The thing that bore deep within my stomach and soured the morning that should have been pleasant. Nothing was coming easy in my brain, and everything fogged, swirling together as I tried to make sense of what I really wanted. Could I have Jack and my dream job? Did I even really have Jack?

Maybe it would be better if I let him find someone else.

Blast.

This would be so much easier if I had someone to talk to. I couldn't talk to Sean since this was his brother. And the only person who I was really close to also happened to be the same person I was debating on leaving or staying with.

I raised my eyebrows, trying to smile at Jack and not think of everything swimming in my brain. "I don't think you need to get anything fancy for Jane Pawsten. She seems to like you without the treats."

He laughed. "Nothing wrong with spoiling my girl."

"Oh, so she's your girl now?" I asked, feeling my chest tighten thinking how ingrained he'd become in my dog's life.

She cried whenever he left and would jump into his arms as soon as we saw him for our nightly walks. She'd never taken a shine to anyone like she did him. If there was one thing I knew about people, it was that if a dog liked them, I trusted them. And that's what gutted me the most. I should have trusted him and told him what my mother said and about the job offer, but I kept both bottled up.

"I already have a dog bowl and leash ready for her at my place. For when she stays the night."

"She might not like that, nor would your neighbors. She'd be up barking and whining all night unless I constantly put my hand near the end of the bed for her to lick my fingers to know I'm there," I said with a smirk, eying some well-worn books as we passed a seller.

"Then you'll just have to come with us."

I blinked and stopped, slowly turning toward him as my heart thudded in my chest. This was definitely more than a euphemism.

"I'm not staying at your place."

He shrugged. "Just an option. If you and Jane ever wanted a change of scenery. The board has always talked about turning your flat and the others in the building into businesses. A boutique publisher would be lovely there. And I know just the girl who could run it."

My mouth dropped open at his proposal and butterflies fluttered in my stomach. A mixture of nerves and, did I dare say, elation?

I may not have known what to think when I talked to Sarah, but when Jack talked about a small publisher in the flat, I immediately thought of transforming the space into a workroom. Exactly how I'd bring in new clients and what kind of books I'd want to publish. I didn't even think that far after reading Carolyn's email.

But it was a silly notion. I couldn't take any of it seriously. This was Jack. This was the guy who needed a wife. Something I didn't want to be. Or so I thought.

But now...now... Now I didn't know what I thought anymore.

"Jack...we...barely..."

His hand clasped mine, stopping my thoughts and sending the butterflies into full spasm mode. "We've known each other for most of our lives, and you said it yourself, your dream is to be a small publisher. You're here, and we both know you're made for so much more than my assistant. I care about you and I want what is best for you.

"I haven't felt like this about anyone. But that has nothing to do with this business idea. It's two separate things. You'll still have the business and the flat. I'll make sure of that. No matter what happens between us."

I couldn't think of a reason to say no.

*The job offer in London.*

*My mother's words.*

*The idea of marriage itself.*

*The company falling into the wrong hands if all of this didn't work out between us.*

Before I could answer, my phone rang. I shook my head, searching through my bag.

A new sense of dread coursed through me, hoping it wasn't Carolyn or Sarah. Not while I was in the middle of this moment with Jack.

But instead of seeing either of their numbers flash across my screen, it was my mum's and I let out a sigh of relief.

"Hello, Mum."

"You're finally not too busy to answer your phone. Does this mean I should expect you for tea this afternoon or do you have one of those work meetings again? You've been having an awful lot of those lately. I hope Jack isn't working you too hard."

I held back my laugh, Jack's eyebrows wiggling as he listened to her words.

"Actually, I'm with him right now. Working, that is," I said quickly.

She huffed. "Oh, well I guess you can invite him, too."

"What?" I asked, my eyebrows raised so high they practically hit my hairline.

"The more, the merrier. I'll make sure to set out an extra plate."

"I…I don't know…he's an awfully busy man," I stammered.

She huffed. "Gracie just invite him. You're a grown woman, and you can do what you want but if you'd like to invite him then be here at half past two."

Did Mum have some ulterior motive in inviting him? Make a fool out of me so he wouldn't try to have a real relationship with me?

This was all bloody complicated and I was probably overthinking it.

I hung up the phone and looked at Jack, chewing on my bottom lip as I chose my words carefully. "Mum wants me to go there for tea. She told me to invite you but I feel like it's probably a cover for something else. Like maybe she wants to see if we're shagging or Grandfather wants to talk to you about business. I don't know."

I blew out a breath, before he could answer, everything coming out like word vomit. "It's up to you. I don't really want to be there, so maybe having you with would be a good excuse to leave early."

I decided that was as good a reason as any. I could use a buffer with my mum, and maybe if he was there, she wouldn't bring up the inheritance clause or her ludicrous plan. The one that she had to realize by now I was never going to do.

I wasn't going to be his forever, his wife.

I just knew that I wasn't ready for my day with him to end. Our time together at all.

I didn't want to think about the email from Carolyn and what my answer would be. Or even what the future would be beyond today. I just wanted to escape all of it with him.

He took my hand and brought it to his lips, brushing his mouth against my knuckles. "As long as you're there, I'll go anywhere."

# Chapter Sixteen

JACK

Much like the Murphys, the Walsh family came from old money.

I knew this because as soon as Seamus retired from the jewelry business, he sold his lavish estate with a gymnasium, indoor swimming pool, multiple sitting rooms, and a golf course.

After uni, I ended up with a semi-detached brick home, much like the one we were pulling up to that the family had downgraded to. By downgrade, I mean the home cost two million euros instead of the twenty million euros his estate went for.

After the market that morning, Grace barely spoke.

"You know, we don't have to do this. I could easily make a very important business call, and we'd have to run to the office. More importantly my desk," I said, squeezing her hand and wiggling my eyebrows.

I didn't fully understand her nerves. We were both adults,

and I'd met her mam and grandparents dozens of times. But this was the first time we'd be with them together like this.

Whatever this was.

"I think we've already been spotted and it's too late for that," she muttered.

I followed her gaze to the window where her mother's head poked through the sheer blinds. As if we didn't spot her, she ducked back from sight.

Grace's face flushed crimson.

"She may have seen that we're here, but that doesn't mean we can't take a quick walk. A shag behind a neighbor's shed, then be on our way," I said, leaning in and keeping my voice low.

An old man with very large jowls opened the door and Grace gasped, jumping back. "Charles," she said, scooting away from me and into the house as if she was on fire.

"Oh, and this is my friend, Jack Murphy. I don't know if you remember him or not," she said, introducing me to the older gentleman.

Charles expression didn't change from his mopey facade, but he nodded. "How do you do, Mr. Murphy?"

"Very well, thank you."

"Madam Evans and Madam Walsh are in the tearoom, this way," he said, ushering us through the foyer and down the gallery hallway filled with oil paintings on the white walls.

The tearoom was one of four sitting rooms we passed. I don't know how Grace's mum got there so fast when we had just seen her, but she was perched in her chair. Next to her was Seamus's wife and Grace's grandmam. The old woman reminded me of a cartoon with her brightly colored dresses and feathered hats. She was a stark contrast against the dark wood floors and white walls of the room.

"Gracie, darling, it's been too long." Elizabeth, Grace's mam, stood up and circled the round table filled with treats, ignoring the maid who was pouring her tea.

Grace gingerly took her mother in an embrace. They kissed each other's cheeks before Elizabeth's dark eyes trailed to me.

I'd first noticed her at the vet's office, but was paying more attention to the dog and not the woman in the uncomfortable looking chair. She was an attractive older woman with her hair in some fancy updo and a flawless face that could have been that of an old British movie star. But if I didn't know any better, I'd say the woman was eyeing me suspiciously like she knew something I didn't.

Had Grace talked to her Mam about me? Seamus knew about the inheritance clause and so did Grace, so in theory, her mother could know. And if she did, did she know there was something going on with the two of us and want something more? Or want me to stay the hell away?

Each new thought made my chest beat with anxiety and I tried not to mull it over. To just live in the moment, in the here and now, and what I had with Grace.

Whatever it was that made all of me feel this alive, at least.

"And Jack, it's been too long. You've been working my daughter so hard. You both could use a break," she said, extending her hand to me. I took her palm gingerly and kissed each of her cheeks before she went back to her seat.

"Grandmum, I believe you remember Jack," Grace said, leaning down and kissing her grandmam's cheek.

"The sexy Irish hunk with a butt like a sailor? Of course, I could never forget him. But it's been a while since I saw him leaving your flat like an escaped convict who just got caught. Come here, boy, lemme get a better look at you," Grace's grandmam commanded, flapping her glove-covered hands.

"Mother," Elizabeth scolded, her face flushing a deep red.

"It's all right," I said, flashing a smile and approaching the old woman, extending my hand.

Grandmum shook her head. "Oh, please, boy, we hug in this family."

She held her arms out and I slowly leaned over, putting my arms gently around the tiny woman. She pulled me close, her lips to my ear. "Don't break her heart, ya hear me? She's really taken a shine to you."

"Don't worry," I whispered, kissing her cheek before I pulled away.

"What was that about?" Grace asked, taking one of the white dining chairs around the table. I sat down next to her.

"It's between me and your grandmum," I said, shooting the old woman a wink.

Two maids circled the table, filling Grace's and my cups with tea and placed plates full of mini sandwiches and fruit in front of us.

"Thank you," I said to the woman pouring my tea. She nodded, not saying a word.

"Eleanor, Elizabeth, you don't expect this lad and me to sit here and discuss matters over tea, do you?" A familiar voice said from behind me.

I didn't need to look to know it was Seamus, who approached the table, leaning on his cane and adjusting his gray toupee.

"A man doesn't need to sit and have tea with the women. Join me for cigars and whiskey in my office," Seamus bellowed, giving me a half-cocked smile. It either said he wanted to enjoy my company or murder me for shagging his granddaughter.

"You don't have to," Grace said, staring at me wide-eyed.

What the hell was that about? Did she need the buffer with her mam that bad?

There was no way in hell the patriarch of the family was

going to let me get away with anything but sitting down with him. And, truth be told, I was more comfortable with the old man than the stares from the women.

"Don't worry, *mo gra*, I won't be long."

She gave me a pointed look that quickly disappeared when I stood and nodded to Seamus, briskly shaking his hand. "Been a while. Haven't had a board meeting yet this month, though a few members have stopped in the office to see the photographs we're adding to the new franchises' decor."

"I've heard about the old photographs from the market. And the men can't stop raving about the cheese and bread. But I've also heard of some other news you might be sharing. Maybe a new endeavor or buying product from a British winery?" He raised his bushy eyebrows.

Ultimately the board would vote on bringing the wine and even the local cheese and bread into the company internationally, but Connor, Sean, and I would veto Lacey's wine. Everything Grace said about the company and her concerns were right. Sean and Connor did another check after our little meeting and made sure of it. That and there was no way in hell I wanted to do a business deal with my ex.

I shot a wink over my shoulder at Grace before the old man and I started down the hallway.

"Mara," Seamus said, stopping a young maid.

"Yes, sir?" she asked.

"Can you get Mr. Murphy and me a bottle of whiskey from the cellar and bring it to my office?" he asked.

"Yes, sir, right away." She scurried off, and I followed Seamus into his office.

While the tearoom was light and airy, all decorated in white, his office was dark and covered in rich mahogany bookshelves and leather furniture around a large oval desk.

He shut the door and walked over to a humidor. He opened it and pulled out two rolled cigars, handing one to me.

"Last time we were in my office together, I believe we were at the old estate. You had just graduated from uni. Thought you were ready to buy my estate and take over the pubs right then and there. Then your da told you the price tag." He laughed, coughing before taking a seat in his chair.

All the men on Murphy's board had the same cough as Da. I didn't think anything of it until the day Da called me into his room and told me he had cancer. I wondered how far off the other men were. Pain twisted my chest, thinking of how much more heartache this family would have to go through if anything happened to the old man.

"Yes, sir, that was my plan. I was just a wet-behind-the-ears kid. But that was years ago, and I think I know a bit more about the company. I've been running it pretty well with Connor and Sean," I said, taking the lighter and slowly igniting Seamus's cigar.

I never smoked the blasted things, but in these sort of settings, I did what the old men did. Even if I just bit down on the end and never actually inhaled. By the sound of Seamus's cough, he shouldn't have been either.

He let out a slow circle of smoke and held the lighter out for me. "You have. But we both know that you can't fully run the place until you and your brothers all have a ring on your finger. Connor already has one; we're all just waiting on you and Sean."

I sucked too hard on the cigar, getting a mouthful of soot and pounded my chest, so I didn't spit everything out on the desk.

"You okay, Jack? Something I said?" He raised an eyebrow.

"Just caught a bit off guard," I said, slowly taking the seat across from him.

He nodded, twirling the brown stick in his hand. "Now that your watch is down, shall we get to the business of why you're here?"

"Pardon, sir?" I feigned innocence but the hair at the nape of my neck stood on end.

"Am I to tell you, a grown man, to not break my granddaughter's heart? No. That's for you and her to decide. But I am telling you, one man to another, that these Evans women may appear tough. They like to hold their heads high, even in the most dire of situations. When they're scared or hurt, they'll put on that tough exterior and do what they have to do. Do you get what I'm saying?"

"That if I hurt your granddaughter, she'll manage but still be wounded?" I asked, trying to understand his analogy. I wanted to tell him that nothing like that was going on with Grace and me, but I couldn't lie to him either. The problem was, I didn't know what exactly was going on between us. The only thing I knew was that I hadn't felt this way about anyone else. Not even Lacey.

"Precisely, my boy. We both know that you have to be married by April. The board has watched you and your brothers flitting about for years. I didn't know you'd end up with my Gracie taking a shine to you. Now tell me, is this going to be the girl you see announcing to the board as Mrs. Murphy?"

I swallowed the lump in my throat, trying to think of the right words to respond. Had I thought about approaching Grace even to see if she wanted to try marriage and get a divorce settlement? Of course. Ever since Sean brought that up in our first meeting with the solicitor, I thought about approaching any girl like that.

But that was before I found out how much her parents' divorce royally fecked her up. How she never wanted to get married.

"With all due respect, sir, Grace and I are just getting to know each other again. I don't want to hurt your granddaughter in any of this. It's not my intention."

He pointed a finger. "Exactly."

"I beg your pardon?" I asked, raising an eyebrow.

"Grace may have started at Murphy with you because I pushed and she needed a job. But you and I both know this isn't her dream job and that she's only doing this temporarily until she finds something else. Hopefully that's in Dublin with us, but that's not the point."

Before I could ask what he meant by that last statement, he continued speaking, shaking his head.

"And you. You're the man who pushes her boundaries. Who makes her go for more. If it weren't for you, she and that dog would still be moping around this house with her mother. I just didn't know there was an actual romance blossoming until now."

The door opened, interrupting us as the maid came in, quiet as a church mouse. She brought a decanter of whiskey to the desk, opening it before pouring two glasses.

Seamus nodded. "If you're going to keep Grace in the business and your heart, just make sure it's for keeps, okay?"

How was I supposed to respond to the man? Did I tell him the confusing thoughts in my mind?

No. That was ridiculous.

The best thing to do was smile and hold my glass. *"Sláinte."*

Luckily Seamus changed the subject off his granddaughter. We talked business for a few beats and finished our cigars. Then we headed back to the tearoom.

The sound of haughty laughter filled the hallway.

I smiled, ready to see Grace and a look of glee on her face. But I stopped short when a fourth chair was filled at the table.

Lacey's blond head tilted back in my direction.

But it wasn't just the girl sitting there, it was the one standing across from her with her eyes wide.

What was Grace going to do now?

# Chapter Seventeen

Mum conveniently left out that Lacey was coming to tea.

It was almost as soon as Jack left with Grandfather that my blonde cousin strutted in, wearing too-high heels and a blue dress that fit way too tightly to be tea appropriate.

There was definitely something conspiring.

While Lacey bent down to hug Grandmum, I glared at Mum, but she just pursed her lips like I should be grateful.

"Gracie, didn't know you were going to be here," Lacey said smugly, kissing my cheek before she sat down.

"Mum called while I was working, but Jack and I were able to take a break," I quipped.

"Working? The two of you together?" Her thin eyebrows shot up.

"Not like that. Work-working. We were actually at the market. Jack found a bread and cheese seller he's thinking of using for the pubs. At least the local pubs, then hopefully, moving onto the rest of the franchises," I said, feeling a sense of pride.

Why the bloody hell was I getting giddy for the company?

Maybe it's because my braggadocious cousin was usually the one to talk all high and mighty.

"Well, isn't that nice. I thought for sure when you two walked into that meeting you were just his little assistant. Then that story about you being head of purchasing. Still something I can't believe. They must be pretty desperate at Murphy's." She gave me a small smile that was strained and full of pity.

"Actually, the company is doing very well and adding another one hundred franchises in the next five to ten years," I said, relived that I had actually read over the quarterly reports.

"Glad that literature degree you have is good for something. Though maybe if it was business and from an English school, you wouldn't have lost that job at whatever that publisher was," she said, waving her hand.

I wanted to toss my hot tea all over her. I probably would have if Grandmum wasn't staring at us with a massive grin on her face and Mum with watchful eyes.

"It's so nice to have all my girls together," Grandmum said, throwing her arms, full of bangles, in the air.

"Mum would have come, but she and father are in Budapest for a charity event this week. They send their love, though," Lacey said, taking her teacup.

Mum's lips tightened. Like my disdain for Lacey, I always thought she had the same disgust for her brother, Lacey's father, Collin. But she never voiced it, and the proper Brit wouldn't in front of company. She would later when she spiked her teacup and cried alone in her room.

Grandmum nodded. "They're very busy people. I understand. Maybe someday we'll all be able to get together. Who knows, maybe we'll even hear wedding bells soon."

"Shite." Wait did I say that out loud?

Lacey laughed so hard she covered her mouth and stifled a snort.

Mum and Grandmum widened their eyes, but I glared pointedly at the blonde wench who was still cackling.

"What's so funny?" I asked through gritted teeth.

"Gracie," Mum warned.

But I didn't budge. I didn't move my stare from Lacey's smirk. I wasn't going to let my cousin get in another dig. If I could stand up to Jack on a daily basis, then I could stand up to this girl, too. Consequences be damned. I had enough shite to deal with and I didn't need to add her.

"The talk of a wedding. From either of us. I mean, my last boyfriend was a wreck, and I don't know if you've dated anyone, ever," she said.

She shook her head. "You're the one who always said you never wanted to be married. Though you did have some moments with your little boy toy friend, Sean Murphy. Is he still around? I heard he was playing some sport now." She laughed again, putting her teacup to her lips like that was the end of our conversation.

"Actually, Sean's a professional rugby player. But he's not my boyfriend. And I am seeing someone," I blurted before I could take back the words.

"Oh? And who would that be? Someone at work? Maybe I know him," she replied smugly.

"Yes. You do. It's Jack Murphy," I blurted, the first time saying out loud that there was something between us. It was like a heavy weight had been lifted off my shoulders.

Lacey laughed harder, clutching her hand to her chest as if I had just said the most ridiculous thing ever. "First the job in purchasing, now you want me to believe you actually landed a man like Jack Murphy? Oh, Gracie, you're sweet, but I'm not daft. No way a man like that would ever fall for you."

Every hair on my arms and the back of my neck stood on end and I sprang from the chair, my fists clenched at my side. "Listen, Lacey, I've put up with your stuck-up attitude for years and I'm sick of it."

"I beg your pardon?" Lacey blinked slowly, her mouth open.

I rolled my eyes. "Oh, come on, don't give me that shite. You think you're better than me, always have, but what you don't know is that I've been with that so-called boyfriend of yours for weeks now. And you know what? We're happy. Really deliriously happy together."

She opened her mouth to speak, but I interrupted.

"You know what else? You may think I'm not good for any sort of work because of a literature degree from a school in Geneva, but Jack saw my degree and work experience then encouraged me to go for other positions. Yes, I was hired as an assistant, but he's done nothing but push me forward. And I'm so damn good at the editor thing, that London wants me back to run a line with the publishing house."

By the time I was done with my tirade and finally let out a breath, a slow clap came from behind Lacey as my sexy man walked into the room.

"Another job offer?" Jack asked, approaching me with the corners of his mouth slightly upturned.

"Yes. But I haven't accepted it yet. I mean it's there…and…"

"Obviously you two aren't that happy if you haven't even told him about another job," Lacey said with a coy smile over her shoulder.

"Oh, feck off, Lacey, this doesn't concern you," I said, still keeping my eyes on Jack. "I just found out."

I wanted to tell him everything that was brewing in me. That I thought about taking the job, but I didn't want to leave him.

But before I could say any of that, Grandmum cleared her throat.

"So, when's the wedding? Or is this just a ruse like you suggested to get the company, Lizzie?" Grandmum's high voice rang in the room and I turned toward her.

My breath caught in my throat and Mum gasped, chiding Grandmum.

I thought this might happen. But not like this. Not in this moment.

Everything moved in slow motion as anger and dread drowned in my brain. There was no going back from this. It was all going to come to a head and in front of my cousin and the man I had fallen for.

The job offer. The inheritance clause. All of it.

Grandmum shrugged, looking between all of us. "What? Isn't that what this is about? The boy wants the company. He either is gonna marry our Gracie, or she's leading him on then gonna break his heart since the girl is never getting married. He won't get the business and Seamus buys it. Isn't that what you told me, Lizzie?"

Jack let go of my hand, balling his in a tight fist. Lacey's smug laugh once again rang in my ears.

The world buzzed around me as I slowly looked to see Jack's face turned downward, his eyes on the ground. "I have a few things I need to catch up on at the office."

"But you two just got here," Grandmum said as if nothing had just happened.

"Thank you for having me. It was lovely to see you all," he said curtly, nodding.

Granddad tried to baffle out a reply, but even he couldn't come up with words. Everyone else stayed silent, their heads down. Even Lacey.

Were they all just going to sit there and let this happen?

"Jack. Wait up," I called, following him to the door,

putting my hand on his as he reached the handle. Blood rushed to my head. The room now spun out of control. I didn't know whether I'd throw up, or cry right there at his feet.

"I'll call you a cab. I assume you'd rather get another ride home," he said gruffly.

I shook my head, my chest aching as I tried to think of the right words. "None of this was ever my intention. You have to know that."

He blew out a breath; his eyes still cast downward. "We don't have to talk about this."

"I think we do," I urged, my voice pleading.

Slowly he turned toward me, his eyes blazing and his jaw clenched. "What do you want me to say? That I'm surprised? I shouldn't be."

I narrowed my eyes, a surge of anger coursing through me. "What the hell is that supposed to mean?"

He shook his head and raked his hand through his hair. "I know you're not the type of girl that would use a man to get his money. At least I never thought you were. But…what they were saying…I know you knew about the inheritance clause. Hell, I told you about it myself. But the rest of it. Was this all a game to you? Is that why you've pushed and pulled so much? Why you kept talking about never wanting to get married? Knowing I'd fall for you anyway and then you'd just leave to take the job in London?"

Tears pricked my eyes, and I had to will them not to fall. My words caught in my throat. There was nothing I could say that would make this situation any better. I couldn't even pretend that my mother's words and ideas hadn't been scrolling through my mind the entire time we'd been together.

"I'll take that silence as a yes," he grumbled before opening the door. "I'll see you at the office on Monday."

The door slammed shut behind him, and I stared at the space he once occupied. His scent still lingered like a whiskey-laid cloud of sadness.

I'd been looking for a sign as to what I was supposed to do with Carolyn's email, and now I had it. But the pain that ached in my heart was at odds with my head once again.

And this time I didn't know which one would win out.

I slowly walked back into the room where Granddad was talking softly to Grandmum.

Lacey was nowhere to be seen, and Mum gulped from her glass that she had probably spiked.

"What the hell just happened there?" I seethed, gripping onto a chair.

"Gracie, you know how Grandmum is. She didn't know..." Granddad started.

"It should have never been brought up by anyone at any time," I snapped, my eyes locked on my mother's downcast ones. "You know she has trouble with reality. She didn't know what she was saying, but you..." I couldn't do this. My mum should have never even brought the subject up.

"What? Are we not going to have a wedding?" Grandmum asked, turning so her large feather hat moved with her.

I shook my head.

Then I grabbed my purse and headed down the back hallway, toward the sunroom with a backdoor that led to the yard.

Before I could even grip the handle, Granddad's cane was right at my heels. He moved awfully fast for a man with bad knees and a new hip.

"Whatever excuse you want to use about my mother's mouth or Grandmum's memory, I don't want to hear it."

Granddad sighed, and I slowly turned toward him.

The past few months he'd looked even older than I remembered him. His wrinkles were deeper and his eyes redder than I'd ever seen.

The man who always stood so tall with a barrel laugh was

now a shadow of his former self. And that feeling of guilt was what made me stand there instead of running outside and never coming back.

"When your mother first heard about the inheritance clause, I knew something was brewing. I just didn't know she actually voiced it to anyone."

I nodded, swallowing the lump in my throat. "I believe you, but that doesn't excuse her."

He shook his head. "No, it doesn't, but I know that what matters now isn't what your mother says, it's what you do. If you want to be with him, you will tell him that none of that was your intention. That maybe you thought you'd never be married, but sometimes love can change that."

*Love?*

That was something that hadn't crossed my mind. Yes, I was starting to care about Jack, but anything more and I'd have to think over the butterflies in my stomach just hearing that word with his name.

"He can't be with me, Granddad. He needs a wife for the company. Grandmum was right that either we'll have to get married or we'll stay together just long enough to break up so he'll lose the company. Nobody wins."

Granddad put his hand on mine. "You both win if it's what you want. What do you want?"

I sighed. "I don't know anymore."

"If you want him, there's no sense in letting him go. Maybe things will work out and he'll fulfill the inheritance clause with you, or not. Sometimes you just have to let fate decide."

I didn't tell Granddad that I thought it was fate that the same day I got an email from my old job was the day all of this went down with Jack.

I had to figure out how to fix this. The problem was that I had absolutely no idea how I was going to do that. I was better at breaking things up than putting them together.

# Chapter Eighteen

I wanted to believe that everything Grace's Grandmum said was a lie. But that combined with her tirade to Lacey, that I didn't hear the beginning of but definitely heard the end with the job offer, and the look on Grace's face when I left said otherwise.

Grace never wanted to get married. She told me that much. And instead of pulling away, I kept pushing forward.

All of this was a way to get back to her job in London. For me to lose the company.

Sitting in my car, I stared at the front door. She'd tried to explain. I wanted to believe her, but the whole thing about leading me on? I had trouble getting past that. Maybe if she'd told me about the job offer.

Instead of the door opening with Grace bounding toward me, a blonde siren came swishing through the back gate.

Her red nails rapped on the window.

I should have ignored her and just drove away. But I

slowly rolled down the window, peering up at her wide eyes and smirk. Guilt roiled deep within my already soured gut.

"Yes?"

"Jack. You and I have history. I was shocked as hell when my cousin informed me she came here with you today. To say I wasn't surprised when Grandmum dropped that bombshell...well, I'd be lying."

I glanced at the house. I half expected to see Grace or her Mam in the window, watching us.

"I don't know what game your family is playing, but I'm not here for anyone and now I'm leaving."

She licked her lips. "My hotel isn't far if you're looking for a place to escape."

I shook my head. The last thing I needed to stop the pang in my chest was her.

"Not a chance in hell, Lacey."

She pulled a small white plastic card out of her pocket, putting it on the seat next to me. "I'm staying in the Merrion suite, Georgian Main House. Plenty of room if you want to sit, have a glass of whiskey and talk, or anything else. No strings. Just me and you reconnecting."

I grabbed the card, holding it out to her. She put her hand on mine, shaking her head.

With Grace, I always felt a warm pulse run through me from a little touch. With Lacey, it was nothing but an icy chill that sent dread further to my gut.

"This isn't about what happened to us in the past or anyone else. This is about you and me relieving some tension in my hotel room. If afterward you want to talk business, we can."

I shook my head, looking toward the window instead of her watchful gaze. "So this is about the wine? I'm sorry, but—"

She squeezed my hand, her long nails digging into my

palm and forcing me to look up at her. "Not wine. The other business."

"We don't have any other business." I swallowed hard, knowing there was more she wanted to get at. The only reason I was still sitting there and not telling her to feck off was because I was waiting to see if anyone else left that house. Particularly the brunette beauty who I'd been spending most of my time with.

Lacey smiled, her red lips curling like a cartoon villain. "You need a wife and what would make a better story than reconnecting with your old school sweetheart? The board would accept that and probably throw us a wedding shower tomorrow."

I sighed, pinching the bridge of my nose, glancing behind her at the still shut front door of the house. "What's in all of this for you?"

"What? Can't a girl just want to connect with her ex and maybe you can help me out with a nice prenuptial agreement in the end? It would be a win-win for both of us," she said, her lips growing more menacing the longer I looked at her.

Pulling my hand back, I opened the passenger side window and chucked the hotel key card to the street. Lacey gasped as I turned back to her.

"No. On the wine, the marriage, or anything else."

She gawked as I rolled the window up then drove off.

I needed whiskey.

· · ·

A half a bottle later, I started to pour myself another glass when there was a knock on my door.

I half expected it to be Grace coming to apologize and my pulse raced at the thought.

*Stupid heart.*

But it was Sean looking at me with a deep scowl.

"Come on in, the whiskey's on the rocks," I slurred, shutting the door before plopping back down on the sofa.

There was nothing warm or inviting about the house I purchased a year ago. The only furniture I had in the living room was the leather sofa that used to be Da's and a flat screen TV on the wall. Well, that and my bar cart with a few bottles of whiskey and some glasses.

"You look like shite, man. I thought I'd see you in a compromising position with Grace, not knackered and watching the telly," Sean said. He sat next to me, practically taking up two spots with his tree trunk legs and biceps.

"Well, Grace had other ideas about our relationship, or whatever the hell I thought we had," I muttered, sipping my drink.

Sean crossed his arms over his chest, turning toward me. "What the feck is that supposed to mean?"

"Hey, she's one of your best mates, surprised she didn't tell you that she, her grandmum, and mum planned on me falling for Grace, only for her to take a job in London and leave. No inheritance clause fulfilled."

Every word dug a knife straight into my gut. I downed the rest of my drink to make the pain go away.

"I don't believe that bullshite for a second," he replied, shaking his head.

I stood up, sauntering toward my bar cart. "Believe it, brother, because I just went through the whole ordeal of Granny going on and on about a ruse to get me to fall for Grace, so Seamus gets the company. That was, of course, after Grace so much as bragged about a job offer in London."

"Nah. You know the old bird has always been out of her mind, hell her crazy hats should say that much," Sean said. "And a job offer in London? It's just that. An offer. She hasn't taken anything."

My body stilled, thinking of Grace's eyes when she couldn't even deny the fact she knew about what her Grandmum was saying. Or that she wasn't going to take the offer. Was this her plan all along? Whatever she was hiding behind the sadness in those caramel-colored eyes of hers, I couldn't tell if it was from regret or what. I just knew that I had to get away.

"Grace didn't deny any of it, either."

He shook his head. "Yeah like she probably denied she was in love with you and saying she never wanted to get married. We both know that's a lie. She may have been right pissed when her parents divorced, but that was before she found you."

"We're not in love. I wasn't the one who hurt her, so if you're thinking about smashing my face, you can save it for the field."

I grabbed another bottle and Sean immediately took it from me, setting it down.

"What the hell, man? Come into my house to take my whiskey. What's next? Are you going to tell me how I shouldn't listen to the ramblings of an old woman? Ignore the girl's own protests of marriage? How even though Grace may be the best thing that ever happened to me, I'm going to throw it all away in a bottle of whiskey?"

He just stared at me.

"I'm just going to sit here, with or without you and my whiskey, and try and forget this all happened."

I slumped down against the stiff leather material.

"And what are you going to do when you go into work on Monday to see your lovely assistant?" Sean asked, his arms thrown out to his side.

I frowned, turning the television up to drown out his words and my own thoughts.

I didn't have an answer. The only thing I could think

about was her warm eyes and red lips. And how her smart mouth was one of my favorite things in life.

"I'll figure it out Monday."

Sean grabbed the remote out of my hands and turned off the TV before chucking it across the room. Once it hit the wall, it broke into half a dozen pieces.

"What the feck?"

"Don't give me some bullshite answers."

I shook my head, my heart beating in my ears. "I'm telling you that I don't know what the feck I'm supposed to do, okay? For once, I have no idea."

"Do you love the company?" he asked, point blank.

I scoffed, resisting the urge to roll my eyes. "Of course, you know that."

"Do you love Grace?"

I swallowed hard, still not knowing the answer to that one.

He blew out a breath. "I don't know how to take your silence, but I will tell you this: if you love the company and if you even remotely care about Grace and the Walsh family, you'll do the right thing."

I laughed, shaking my head, but there was absolutely no humor in my voice or thoughts. "And what exactly is the right thing?"

"I guess you'll know on Monday, won't you?"

# Chapter Nineteen

GRACE

I woke up the next morning with a killer headache from a bottle of wine and a whole lot of crying.

Why the hell was I crying?

I wasn't the type of girl who sobbed over a man. A man who I said I was never going to marry when he needed a wife.

Blast.

I told him that I was never going to get married, yet that didn't stop him. He wasn't pushing me. He spent time with Jane and me, making me forget all about why I was opposed to marriage in the first place.

But when I finally mustered up the courage to go after Jack and tell him that I didn't want to lose him, that I may have been against marriage but for him… That's when it all blew up.

Blast.

I saw Lacey at his car window, her hand on his. All resolve left me and I tried not to cry right there.

I guess I didn't have to worry about Jack moving on and the company being fine without me.

The thought of that panged my already aching chest and head. Would I have to go to every family function and see them so happy together?

Now I was in the present, trying not to worry about the future. But I kept thinking about what could have been. If I didn't bring up the London job in front of Lacey. Then Grandmum wouldn't have said anything.

The buzzing of my phone didn't help my headache, it took everything in my power to move and grab it.

I figured it was probably Sarah or maybe even Carolyn calling about the new position. I didn't know my fate at Murphy's Pub, and there was no way in hell I was going to try a small press on my own. There was no other choice but to take Carolyn's offer and to get the hell out of Dublin.

I managed to clear my throat before answering the phone, not even looking at the screen to see who the caller was. "Hello?"

"Gracie, love, I'm sorry did I wake you?" Mum's almost-too-cheery-voice carried through the speaker.

I shook my head, slowly sitting up. Was she seriously asking that right now? After yesterday? "No, no. I've been up, just doing some yoga."

I stared at Janey's bed and the yoga mat she'd been using as a pillow for a few months.

"Gracie, I know that sleepy voice and that you're still in bed. Granddad wanted me to call to invite you and Jack for dinner and a round of golf tonight. He assumes that Jack golfs, at least."

I sighed, remembering that he did used to golf when we were in school. With Lacey. The girl he was obviously going to go back to.

"We didn't make up yesterday. He left and I'm pretty

sure Lacey left with him," I said, straightening my shoulders.

I didn't wait to see if she did.

"Oh," Mum said, leaving the air thick between us.

"I did really like him," I said. "This wasn't just about trying to convince him to fall for me or chase after me. He'll probably never speak to me again after the fiasco with Grandmum. Why would you ever say something like that? You know how she is." I sighed.

"I never thought—this isn't my fault," Mum said through her teeth.

"I don't even know if it's worth it. He obviously doesn't care about me. And I really was offered a position as an editorial director back in London. A dream job. So, there is that," I blurted quickly.

"I guess some congratulations are in order," she replied, but there was nothing happy in her voice.

I groaned. "Out with it, Mum. I know that tone, and I know the disappointment. I know you wanted this grand ordeal so Granddad could get the company or get me to marry Jack so I could have us all set. Well, none of that happened. I want to be upset with you and Grandmum. But this is on me for not being completely honest in the beginning. I should have told him everything. Not just that I wasn't sure about marriage, but about what you knew."

Mom's voice softened. "Gracie, if I would have known Grandmum would have said all of that, Granddad and I would have never said a word to her. Though, we should have known better."

"Too late now," I muttered.

She sighed. "You know, Lacey confided in me that she broke it off with Jack in uni because he was always so focused on work. She wanted to go back to London and he always had his sights set on running the company."

I had a hard time believing that Lacey would confide in

anyone. "Really?"

Mum laughed. "Well, this was after a few glasses of wine one night, but yes, she did admit that. But what she would never admit was that Jack never looked at her the way he looks at you. The man never made time to meet her family or stop in for tea or whiskey with Grandfather."

"Why are you telling me all of this, Mum?" I asked, wanting her to just get to the point.

"I want you to be happy. Maybe going back to London and taking that job will do that for you. Or maybe, you'll take the job that Grandfather tells me about in purchasing at Murphy's Pub and see where things go with Jack."

"I should get ready. I'll call you later," I said quickly, the tension rising in my temples.

"Okay, let me know if you need anything."

"I will. Thank you, bye."

I sighed and finally got up, walking the few steps to the living room where Jane Pawsten was happily chewing on something near the couch.

"You're not eating another blanket are you girl?" I groaned, crouching down and petting behind her ears.

She happily rolled over for me to scratch her belly, dropping the now half-chewed tie of Jack's. I held up the blue material and found myself half smiling, half in tears, which caused a head tilt from Jane.

I didn't know when he left it at my place, but I remembered how I thought it brought out the blue in his eyes. How much I loved staring at them. The ones that were probably now gazing lovingly at my cousin instead of me.

"Do we go back to London or do we stay here and take a chance?" I whispered.

She didn't say anything and nuzzled into my lap.

I didn't expect a dog to have the answers. But having her there to comfort me was more than I could have asked for.

Then my phone rang, causing Janey to stir in my lap. Fallon's number flashed across the screen.

Shite, was this them sending the cavalry after me?

Quickly I cleared my throat and answered, "Hello?"

"Grace, how are you?"

"Um. I'm grand, you?" I asked tentatively.

"Well, my lovely husband likes to inform me of things at the last minute sometimes, and I found out we have a trip to another Murphy's next week in Boston. I need to do some shopping for the trip and thought maybe you'd want to come with. Connor insisted on a personal shopper, but I'd rather just have another girl go with me. I'm not being too forward, am I?"

Usually, I loved listening to Fallon's incessant rambling, but today it just made the pain tighter in my chest.

"I'd love to, Fal. But I'm not feeling too well. I think it's the flu."

"Oh. I'm so sorry. Do you need me to bring anything? I don't know if they have Tamiflu at the drugstores here, but I can find something."

"No. No. Wouldn't want you getting sick either. I'll just make some tea and stay in bed."

She sighed. "Okay, well maybe when you feel better we can do something. Hopefully, you'll be good for work tomorrow. I think Aileen would cry if I made her sit at your desk."

"Yeah...hopefully I am..." I muttered.

I had one day to decide if I was going to stay at Murphy's or go back to London.

And hopefully I made the right choice.

# Chapter Twenty

Jack

Instead of burying my sorrows and trying not to face Grace at the office, I decided it was better to drown myself in work.

That and I was out of whiskey, so I had to leave the house at some point.

Monday morning, I was greeted by Fallon, sitting in her old seat, smiling.

"Morning, Jack. Thought you might have the flu like Grace."

I froze. Just hearing her name sent my stomach bottoming out.

She couldn't bear to face me, either. I thought the sassy girl would march in and tell me what's what.

The woman who had let her guard down when she was in my arms was now afraid to even see me.

"I'm fine. Make sure all of my calls go directly to my office." I barked, before slamming my door behind me.

I hung my suit coat up on the hook then sat down in my

desk chair. While my computer booted up, I reached into my bottom drawer, where I knew I always had a bottle of whiskey on hand for guests, and late nights.

When I grabbed for one of my rocks glasses, my fingertips ran along the seam of a hidden drawer, one I'd almost forgotten about.

When I first moved into this office, when Da got sick, I found his whiskey bottle easily. But this hidden drawer wasn't something I had expected.

Like a glutton for punishment, I opened the small drawer, pulled out the black velvet box, and opened the clasp. Inside was an emerald and diamond ring, set in a gold band with Celtic knots molded into the metal.

It was my grandmam's, and when Mam passed, Da must have stored it here.

I stared at the jewelry and thought of what I'd just lost.

I'd never fallen so hard and fast for anyone.

"Brother. Good to see you're in early as usual," Connor said.

I didn't hear him come in until it was too late, and I couldn't hide the ring box.

His eyes widened as he approached my desk, slowly circling until he was looking down at me. "Is that what I think it is? You're ready to propose?"

I shook my head. "No. I'm nowhere close to proposing to anyone. This was Grandmam's ring and then Mam's. I found it a while ago in Da's drawer and almost forgot about it until I was looking for some whiskey."

"What?" he asked, shaking his head as he leaned against my desk, crossing his arms over his chest.

I thought maybe Sean had spoken to him, but if he did, Connor wasn't letting on.

I closed the ring box, putting it back in the drawer before I pulled out the bottle and two glasses. "This probably needs a drink for me to explain."

"That bad that we should be drinking at eight in the morning?" he asked as I poured each of our glasses.

I quickly summed up tea at Grace's grandparents and how it ended with her talking about a job in London and her grandmum. Once I finished, I stared at our full glasses, the liquid no longer looking enticing.

"That's some bullshite," he replied.

"You're telling me."

"So what are you going to do about it?" He asked, drumming his fingers on the desk.

I frowned. "What do you mean, 'what am I going to do'? I really cared for the girl, and when all that came out, she didn't deny it. She didn't look pleased, though. Maybe I'm not meant for any of this marriage stuff. I should just find a woman to partner with so we can get the company then divorce her with a settlement. That's all I'm meant for."

"You know we're not all destined to be alone like Da," Connor said, resting his hands on his lap.

I didn't respond and leaned back in my chair. So he was right about drinking at eight a.m., though that was the only thing that I thought could dull the pain in my head. To get me not to think about the one who got away.

"Da always talked about how important family was to him, even though he sent us off to boarding school and he never married anyone else," Connor said. "I think he put that clause in because he wanted us to be happy. To be better than him. I think he wanted to give us that push to find love for real."

I smirked. "Don't go rubbing you and Fallon in my face now."

He shook his head. "I'm just saying that when I first met Fallon, I didn't think she was going to be my forever love. It wasn't until it was almost too late that I realized I couldn't be without her. After her ex showed up at our wedding, I almost did. But I couldn't let her go. Do the same, Brother."

"You think that I should just ignore what happened? Tell her I do have feelings for her? That I want to see if this works out and if it doesn't, well, then screw the company?" I raised an eyebrow.

He nodded, standing up from my desk. "We all do crazy things or say stupid stuff in the moment. What matters is our actions after the fact."

"You're saying I should show up at her flat and grovel? Tell her all of this?" I barked.

He shrugged, already heading for the door. "That's for you to figure out. Not me. But I can say, I know you've been in love with the girl since you saved her and Sean's asses from being arrested when they were teens."

I shook my head, the thought of that even preposterous. We had hated each other. "Are you mad?"

He laughed. "No, I think for the first time, in a long time, I'm finally seeing things. If it were any other girl Sean was calling you about to come to the rescue, you would have told him to feck off. But you didn't because it was Grace."

"That was years ago. I didn't know my head from my arse back then," I muttered, trying not to think on Connor's words.

It was true. I remember being in the middle of a date with a fairly nice bird. But I immediately jumped in to help Sean and Grace. I told myself it was because he was my brother and she his friend. But Connor's words made sense.

Bloody hell.

Had I really always had these feelings for her? My heart raced at the thought.

I groaned, leaning my head back against the chair. Now I knew things were more fecked up than I had originally thought.

"Call me if you need a ride to her flat or to have Fallon order flowers," Connor said before he shut the door, leaving me in an ominous silence.

A new email notification *pinged* on my computer. At least work could keep my mind busy while I figured this out.

Opening up the app, my fingers froze over the keys as I read the words on the screen. The ones that would be ingrained in my memory forever.

*Jack,*

*You're either at work or probably still in bed with my cousin. Yes, I did see her outside, leaning over your car when I was going after you. I wanted to tell you that, yes, Mum did suggest all of that, but I never thought of any of it. I told her she was nuts for even thinking it.*

*I think I kept pushing you away because I didn't want you to think I was only with you for the company. The more I pushed, the harder I fell. And I did fall hard for you. I don't blame you for being angry, but it did hurt that you would think I would do anything to cause you harm.*

*I think it's best for us to end this working relationship.*

*I took the job back in London, so I've booked a flight to Heathrow. I'll be out of the flat and your life soon.*

*Though I'm gone, know that I did care about you, Jack. Whether you believe me or not I'll miss you, and I'll always treasure the time we had together.*

*Grace*

If my chest wasn't already aching, now it shattered into a

million pieces.

I was an arse. There was no way she would have done what her grandmum had said. I should have known that.

*Feck.*

What the hell was I supposed to do now?

I couldn't just show up at the airport with flowers and beg for forgiveness.

I looked again at the velvet box.

All of this started, I thought, when I approached the girl in the red dress at the gala.

But now I knew better.

This was the girl I was always supposed to be with. The one who made me a better man like Da wanted us to be when he made out that will. I just never saw it before. Until her.

But she was gone and all I had left was whiskey, memories, and a still looming deadline.

Worst of all, I missed her and that damn dog so much.

I had to fix this.

As if Fallon knew, she knocked on the door before opening it without an answer.

"Jack?" she asked tentatively.

"Whatever Connor told you to do, don't do it," I grumbled.

She laughed, walking the few steps to my desk. "Then it's a good thing I don't listen to him."

I raised an eyebrow.

"I have a feeling by the heated discussion in here that Grace doesn't have the flu."

I rolled my eyes. "Fallon, I love you, but I don't exactly want relationship advice from anyone right now."

She plopped a white envelope on my desk and I stared from the paper back to her. "Then it's a good thing I'm not giving it."

"What is this?"

"I have access to your emails still, too. You know what

you need to do and if you're going to open that envelope and do it, that's on you. I'm not giving you advice, I'm giving you the tools you need to go for what you want."

I picked up the envelope, though it was light, the weight of it felt as heavy as my heart.

"You're as mad as my brother," I said, shaking my head with a whisper, pins and needles pricking my skin.

"Yeah, we may be. But we also know when we're right."

# Chapter Twenty-One

I'd never quit a job before. There was probably some sort of protocol and HR would have a lot of questions about my email to Jack.

But I didn't care.

It was what I had to say. The only way I could do that was with the written word.

I'd never been good at expressing my emotions. I could have blamed that on my cold upbringing, but the truth of the matter was, I was good at shutting people out. It was what I did.

Jack was the first person to ever make me want more.

But now I couldn't face him. Not after what I'd done.

As I was leaving the flat, I saw a small stand that was selling Magic Stars. I had to bite my lip to hold back my emotion.

I made my way to the waiting cab, forcing my stupid feelings down.

Several minutes later we arrived at the airport. After checking in, I found the first bar I could.

The bartender peered at me, cleaning a wineglass. "What'll be, ma'am?"

I looked at the array of bottles behind him, but one clearly caught my eye. And, like a glutton for punishment, I pointed at the bright green bottle.

"Some of the Murphy's whiskey, please," I said, setting Jane Pawsten and her crate at my feet before hopping on the barstool.

"Straight up? Or in a cocktail?" he asked.

I glanced at the laminated menu on the counter. There were millions of different cocktail recipes, and I knew nothing about whiskey, even after my time with Murphy's.

"Just on the rocks, please," I said, putting down the menu and trying to focus on anything but my thoughts of Jack.

He nodded. "Coming right up."

Pulling my phone out of my purse, I refreshed my emails. I'd sent the letter to him this morning, but I still hadn't heard anything. I guess this was my sign that going back to London was what I was supposed to do.

I'm pretty sure my broken heart sighed a little.

Jane Pawsten stirred in her case before she started barking loudly, causing the other patrons to stare and grimace.

"Janey," I hissed, looking down at the now moving case. At this rate she would be across the terminal, still in the cage.

I hopped off the stool and opened the little door, with every intention of holding her and calming her down, or at least trying to. But instead of grabbing her, as soon as the zipper was undone, she pounced out of the bag and bolted away from the bar.

"Janey," I yelled, following her with my eyes as she landed right in the arms of a well-dressed man with a dimpled smile, crouching down in front of her.

My breath caught in my throat as I slowly approached them.

"Hi, Jane Pawsten, girl, I've missed you," he said, petting behind her ears.

My formerly steady beating heart was now going at warp speed.

I never thought I'd hear his beautiful Irish accent again, but here he was. Jack Murphy was in the airport, petting my dog. Making my heart do things I never ever thought it would do.

He kept his eyes on Jane Pawsten. "I was never a dog person. Never thought I'd want to own one and always told people I didn't like animals. Then I met you and you changed all of that."

"You can't have my dog," I said, my voice cracking.

He finally looked up, his beautiful blue eyes finding mine. All of the warmth that had left my body when he had left now flooded back. "I don't want just your dog, *mo gra*. I want everything that comes with her. Especially you. The woman who is the best thing that ever happened to me."

"What are you doing here? I thought you'd be with Lacey."

He shook his head. "No, not that the bird didn't try. I left her standing in front of your grandparents' house. You are the only woman for me. And it took me too damn long to realize it." He stood up slowly, holding Janey in his arms. "I don't want you to take that job in London. I need you both here with me. And not just for the company."

My hand warmed as he took it in his. "What we both said can't be changed. I know you don't want to be married, and I can't fault you for that. Maybe I'm crazy for being here right now, but I also know I'd be an absolute idiot if I let the first girl to capture my heart go. I can't lose you, *mi stolin*. I love you too much."

*Love.* That wasn't a word I'd said to anyone, but now with Jack, I knew that was exactly how I felt.

"I love you, too," I murmured.

A wide grin spread across his face as he pulled me close, Jane Pawsten not even stirring in his arms. "No more secrets. No more assumptions. Okay?"

He pushed a stray strand of my hair behind my ear and my heart beat faster and slower at the same time. "As long as I can have you again, I don't want to worry about inheritance clauses or anything else. Just us."

My cheeks burned, and my mind said that maybe I should wait. But my heart knew better, it always had. "Well, it's too bad that I just quit my job at a big pub franchise and don't have a place to stay. Maybe you know someone who can help me?"

If it was possible, the grin widened. My body turned into a complete puddle of goo. "I may know a franchise heir with a house, perfect for a dog, and some office space that could be used to set up a small press."

I smiled, finally, and leaned into him. "Maybe if you have a salmon ladder back at that place of yours, we can talk."

He put his arms around my waist and pulled me against his hard body. "As long as you don't spill a drink on me."

With that, I did the only thing that was left to do and kissed him. I poured all of my love and happiness into his lips, not caring that we were in the middle of an airport or that Jane Pawsten was barking in his arms.

This all started with a spilled drink and a red dress.

But this was my man.

And this time, I wasn't letting him go.

# Epilogue

I'd never wanted to get married.

Then Jack Murphy hit on me at a gala, and my life had never been the same.

"We should get married," I murmured, lying in bed next to him and intertwining our fingers.

His eyes widened and I swallowed hard, the fear of rejection sinking in my gut.

"You're serious? I thought you never wanted to…"

I sighed, rolling onto my back and pulling the sheet over my chest. "I didn't. But you need to get married for the company, and I love you. We're practically living together as it is, why not just make the leap?"

He shook his head and slowly sat up.

My chest tightened and I clenched the sheet in my fists.

Crap. I put my heart out there and now he was going to reject me?

He leaned over the bed, riffling through his trouser

pockets before sitting down.

Or I thought he was sitting down until I finally looked over. My breath caught in my throat when I sat up and found him down on one knee, holding a small black box.

"I've been carrying this thing around since the day you left for the airport. I knew I'd propose to you. I didn't know when or how, but of course your stubborn arse tried to do it before I could."

"Jack…"

He shook his head, opening the box to reveal a sparkling diamond ring inside. "We can argue about this forever and we probably will. But you're the only woman I want to argue with forever."

Tears stung my eyes and I wiped them away.

He frowned and stood up slowly before sitting on the bed. His hand went to my cheek, brushing a tear away with the pad of his thumb. "Too much, *mo chroí*?"

I sniffled. "I'm not crying because I'm sad. I'm truly happy."

"So is that a yes? You'll marry me?"

I smiled, taking his hand and kissing his palm. "I believe I asked you first."

He laughed, grabbing me around the waist and pulling me close. "Did anyone ever tell you you're a right pain in the arse? But you're my pain, and yes I'll marry you if you'll have me."

As if she knew she was interrupting a tender moment, Jane Pawsten barked from the floor, jumping so I could see the tops of her little ears.

Jack leaned over and with one hand, scooped up the little furball, putting her on the bed next to us.

I looked over at Jane, scratching behind her ears. "What do you say, Jane Pawsten? Think we should give up this whole 'never getting married thing'?"

She barked, turning in a small circle before curling on the bed next to us.

"I don't speak dog, but I'm thinking that's a yes," Jack said, one hand on my waist and the other on Jane's back.

I met Jack's eyes, smiling as my heart beat wildly. "We both say yes."

• • •

I wanted to call everyone and tell them the good news right away, but Jack agreed it would be better at brunch with my family there, and of course his brother, Sean.

My hands slightly shook as we walked through the long hallway toward the dining room.

"Nervous?" Jack asked.

"A little. I mean, this is a big deal and what if they all just think this is really a ruse or Mum hates me for marrying you or…"

He sealed his lips over mine before I could do any more protesting.

I just wanted to get lost in his kiss and savor the moment, but Jane barked at our feet, prying us a part. And I knew we had to face my family.

And his, for that matter.

As soon as we entered the dining room Granddad's voice boomed, "And here's the happy couple. Have something to say to us?"

My eyes widened as I turned to Jack who grinned. "What? Did you really think I'd ask you without getting your grandda's permission first?"

"You wanker." I squeezed his hand but couldn't hide the elation in my voice.

Sean was the first one to stand from the table and give me a huge hug, lifting me off the ground to spin me before setting me back to the floor. "So I guess I get to call you sister now?"

He raised his eyebrows but then lowered them, narrowing

his eyes at his brother. "Still stands that if you hurt her, I'll kill you. Brother or not."

Jack shook his head. "Wouldn't dream of it. Now just to get you married off."

Sean muttered something under his breath I couldn't hear before the two brothers hugged. Then we went around the table getting congratulatory hugs from the rest of the family with Mum being the last one.

I held my breath as she slowly approached us.

"I just want to say...I'm happy this is how everything turned out," Mum said. "Truly. I'm so sorry for any trouble I caused."

I shook my head, glancing at Sean who stood to the side of us with his brows furrowed in question. "Mum, it's fine..."

He was looking to play my bodyguard as always. But before he could approach us, Jack lifted his hand as if to say *I got this*.

Sean glanced at me then looked back to his brother with a curt nod.

"No. It's not fine," Mom quipped as I zeroed my attention back on her. "What your father did to this family put me in an awful place, one I shouldn't have dragged you into. For that, I'm sorry, to you and your future husband."

Her eyes flickered down then back to us, tears brimming. She'd always tried to hide her feelings from the world. That show of emotion nearly did me in.

Jack smiled, putting an arm around Mum. I had to swipe under my eyes to make sure I didn't turn into a blubbering mess right there.

"Everything happens for a reason, and all that matters is that we're all here now. Right where we're supposed to be," Jack said softly before kissing her cheek and shooting a wink in my direction.

Sean's booming voice called over Mum's shoulder,

knocking us out of our happy little family moment. "Since this is a celebration now, does this mean we're getting out the whiskey?"

Jack rolled his eyes, and I laughed. Each Murphy was more of a pain than the last. But they were my pains.

There were looming deadlines and a wedding to plan, but for once it was just about Jack and me. We had the rest of our lives to worry about the company and the family.

# Acknowledgments

First and foremost, to everyone who picked up *Straight Up Irish* and begged me to keep writing: You're the backbone of these stories and what keep me going!

Big thanks to my agent, Stephanie with SBR Media for believing in me and this project when I didn't want to keep writing. Her southern mama sass will make anyone work.

My amazing editor, Candace, who still refuses to use the term Alicorn but since she let me keep the salmon ladder scene, all is forgiven.

Big ups to my Entangled publicists and #TeamIrish, Holly and Riki. Thanks for putting up with my crazy.

Emersyn Vallis, Cat Mason, Angel Justice, Laura Ward, Misha Elliot, Kristen Johnson, and Lauren Fitch. Thank you all for reading and giving me feedback to make this story great even with 500,000 re-writes.

My Social Butterfly publicist, Emily, for believing in my stories even before I was a client.

The cast of *Descendants* and *Black Panther*: without these movies for my kids to watch over and over, this book would have never been completed.

Michelle, my Irish mo gra, thanks for keeping me bloody Irish.

My #FEELTHEVERN and #INSTAVERN teams. Thanks for always having my back and reading my stories.

Twothy, Liv, and Claire Bear. Thanks for loving me and my stories no matter what. Even if you think they sound boring. I love you all to the moon and back.

# About the Author

Magan Vernon has been living off of reader tears since she wrote her first short story in 2004. She now spends her time killing off fictional characters, pretending to plot while she really just watches Netflix, and she tries to do this all while her two young children run amok around her Texas ranch. Find her online at www.maganvernon.com

*Discover the* **Murphy Brothers** *series…*

STRAIGHT UP IRISH

*Discover more New Adult titles from Entangled Embrace...*

## BIG STICK
### a novel by R. C. Stephens

Hockey is my life. And it's a great one. Everything is perfect until she shows up. Oli's twin sister, Flynn...hates my guts. I'm part of one of the worst nights of her life. The way she looks at me sometimes, well, let's just say my hockey stick isn't the only thing that's feeling hard these days. But if she finds out the secrets I'm keeping, forgiveness will be the last thing on her mind.

## UNTIL WE'RE MORE
### a *Fighting for Her* novel by Cindi Madsen

Chelsea is the best friend I've ever had. Ever since she left, I've been a wreck, focusing only on keeping my family's MMA gym afloat. But now she's finally back, and things are weird between us. By weird, I mean I can't stop thinking about her in *that* way. Even stranger, I'm pretty sure she's feeling the same. And this time, I'm not going to stop fighting until we're more.

## Once Upon a Player
### a *British Bad Boys* novel by Christina Phillips

When my mum gets sick, I volunteer to fill in for her and clean some hot jock's penthouse. I've heard all the rumors about him, so the plan is get in, clean some toilet bowls, and get out. After my last experience with a "sports hero," I'm done with that sort of guy. Unfortunately, spending time with Lucas Carter is dangerous. He's so charming, but I can't let myself forget––once a player, always a player.

## Unfixable
### by Tessa Bailey

Willa Peet isn't interested in love. She's been there, done that, and has the shattered heart to prove it. Ready to shake the breakup, she heads to Dublin, Ireland. But there's a problem. A dark-haired, blue-eyed problem with a bad attitude that rivals her own. And he's not doling out friendly Irish welcomes. Shane Claymore is only in Dublin long enough to sell the Claymore Inn and get things in order for his mother and younger sister. Meeting a sarcastic American girl makes him question everything, but will their pasts destroy any hope of a future together?

Made in the USA
Columbia, SC
03 April 2019